D1374884

An EnterTaining Anthology

Tain Writing Group

Edited by Clio Gray & Dave Smith

Copyright © 2016 Tain Writing Group
All rights reserved.
ISBN: 1535227680
ISBN-13: 978-1535227681

DEDICATION

To all aspiring writers everywhere.

This is what can be achieved by dedication, hard
work
& being open to criticism.

We would also like to thank Highlife Highland,
the Highland Library Service and The You Time
Partnership Project who have made this
anthology possible.

CONTENTS

Introduction

It has been my pleasure over the past two years to have given Creative Writing Workshops in Tain Library, in partnership with the Highlife Highland You Time initiative. My aim was to give people space and inspiration, give them time to actually sit down and write. And many of the pieces created in those sessions are featured here. We used snatches of poetry, paintings, images, brief outline scenarios to spark off ideas in our writers, and the resulting breadth and scope of their work is remarkable.

I hope you agree.

Clio Gray

About Our Writers

Bryan Rowe

Throughout my working life all my writing has been mainly confined to completing Professional Reports and Secretarial duties for Local Organisations. Now I am retired I have found a new lease of life in developing Creative Writing skills as a source of inspiration for short story writing and writing my first novel.

Living in the Tain area, it has been a privilege over recent months to participate in Creative Writing courses and personally meet with both experienced authors and new writers and share in their varied knowledge and experiences of writing for pleasure.

Pam Rowe

I am retired and have enjoyed the Creative Writing course immensely as I am 74 years old and fairly handicapped, and feel that it has been something I can participate in and achieve a goal of improving my writing ability so that I can fulfil a lifelong ambition of writing a novel.

The course was very challenging, but I've have learnt a lot under the support and tuition given by Clio.

Debbie Ruppenthal

Debbie was given her first typewriter at the age of 11 and has been writing prose, poetry and short stories ever since.

Born in London, but now living on a hill overlooking the Cromarty Firth, Debbie was a founder member of Inverness Highland Literary Salon. having spent the last decade working in the third sector, she now works as a self-employed cook. An enthusiastic blogger and writer, Debbie enjoys photography, arts and crafts, gardening, and is a keen proponent of all things 'green'.

Jane Marie MacGillivray

Jane Marie lives on a farm nearby Tain, and gets great satisfaction from writing and illustrating, when she can discipline herself to sit down and focus on it, without getting-up to roast something for her large family to eat at regular intervals. She has a BA degree, and has aspirations to further her studies, and to finish her first novel by next Spring.

Josephine Sumner

Josephine has lived in the Highlands for many years and has always enjoyed writing. She has had several short stories and poems published, and one of her plays has been performed in Edinburgh.

Rebecca Nankivell

Rebecca loves writing, but finds it hard to find the time. She has a fascination with China, ever since visiting it several years ago. She is incorporating those experiences into her first novel.

Kenneth Blyth

As a history graduate, who has spent the better part of twenty years absorbing sci fi and fantasy stories in all their mediums, I thought it might be worth putting some of my own ideas down.

Laura Kirk

Laura is still attending Tain Royal Academy and is our youngest contributor.

Aw Mee Wee Lee Ar? *Have you eaten yet?*

(A traditional and common Karen greeting)

By Debbie Ruppenthal

JamYang hunched forward, arms on knees. He was aware of the crawling flies, the piss and the sweat, the dryness in his mouth, the throbbing in his head, the bare grey concrete of floor and walls, the single naked light bulb and the small high-up single paned window; but his mind was blank.

He knew, though, that he had to sit up, mustn't look defeated.

Slowly he inched himself upwards, felt the greasy slide of sweat. He got upright, shoulders slouched, head dipped.

He couldn't make sense of it, of why he was here – or how long. A few days? A week? And why hadn't they tortured him? They hadn't even taken his ring or his Kayan bracelet. He tried to puzzle it out but it was too exhausting.

He groaned inwardly, tried to raise a hand to push the flies from his arm. He didn't have the energy, didn't have the energy to do anything except stare ahead and keep himself from

1

sliding off the stool.

And then he heard them – boots on concrete approaching the room; sound of metal scraping – locks and bolts being undone – and then they were closer. Right outside his door, yanking it open. An SDPC (State Peace and Development Council -Government) official looking up before him, yelling at him in English.

'Where is she? Tell us where she is and we let you go.'

JamYang shivered in spite of the heat. He tried to understand the words – he was fluent in Burmese and Karen too, but his English wasn't as good. What were they were asking him? What girl? Who were they...?

The baton struck him hard on the shoulder, pain sudden and immediate as a lightning bolt. He crumpled forward, biting his tongue so he wouldn't cry out. Needing to think beyond the pain.

'Is she in Thailand?' the guard barked. 'Has coward crossed the border yet? We've other ways to find her; you may as well tell us, Jam Yang. Yes, we know your name. We know all about you.'

JamYang's brain was playing its internal cinema again: the village burning, the army shooting the villagers as they ran, Zoya being dragged away by the KNLA (Karen National Liberation Army -anti Government Forces). Across the border to safety? Yes, he thought so. And he hid for days, a bullet in his arm, without food and water, clinging to life, hoping some of the others were still alive too...

The guard prodded him in the bollocks with the end of the baton. He turned the corners of his mouth into a forced smile. 'Ha! Kalar (derogatory Burmese word for 'black-skinned' people or 'undesirable aliens') You won't be needing these much, eh? All your women gone to camps in Thailand' He prodded JamYang's bollocks again and laughed.

JamYang was shaking now, sweating even more. How was that possible, he wondered, unable to fix his mind on the guard, the baton. Pain. In his groin. In his head. Pain in his whole body, far worse than the bullet wound had been. And then. Nothing.

He woke, prostrate on the cold concrete floor, instantly aware of the pain in his groin, one testicle swollen to the size of a winter melon. He grimaced as he moved his leg. He hadn't told them anything. Yet. Could he hold out, or would he die here without anyone knowing where he was? He couldn't think about that. He had to hold on. If they knew where Zoya was they wouldn't be questioning him. He had to believe that.

The window was jungle-dark, no light from stars or moon. The electric light hurt his eyes, making his head throb as he looked towards the glaring bulb. He strained to hear. No boots. No metal on metal. He pushed himself painfully up and propped his sticky back against the cold grey concrete wall and shuddered. What was that noise in his head? JamYang tipped his head from side to side, then realised the noise was coming from outside. Rain. Coursing down in torrents on the tin roof, rushing down the building in strident waterfalls. He wanted to embrace the rain, to quench himself with it, to worship the river spirit of his ancestors.

'What strange thoughts, JamYang, when you have no land to worship your gods on, when you are almost certain to die in a concrete hut in the jungle! And now you talk to yourself!'

JamYang jerked his gaze to the uneven floor as something caught his eye: a large jewel beetle was tapping its way across the floor, its casing glinting like rubies and emeralds in the harsh electric gleam. As he pondered where the bejewelled creature had come from a deafening blast rocked the building. A shimmer of fine grey dust coated his clammy body as the ceiling cracked, and two of the walls crumbled into the room. Dazed and afraid, JamYang was unable to react, unable to move.

It might have been minutes later, or hours. JamYang took in the rubble that had been his prison. The noise of the wind was deafening, shaking what trees remained, lashing rain in torrents across the jungle clearing. There was no sign of his captors. His head was pounding and the pain in his bollocks stopped him from thinking straight. A cyclone. It had to be. He dragged his way across what remained of the room and tried to heave himself up on the rubble. Too weak, he collapsed into the heap, scudding his forearms and shins on the rough stone and cement.

'Huh! At least you will die a warrior and a man.'

He hadn't heard the approach in the din, but he saw the glint of metal behind the trees. So, he would die at their hands after all. He closed his eyes and waited for the gunfire.

'Aw mee wee lee ar? Aw mee wee lee ar?'

Loud insistent voices hammered in his head and someone was shaking him violently. He opened one eye cautiously, placed a hand across his groin.

'Aw mee wee lee ar, JamYang?'

They knew his name. He opened both eyes as wide as his swollen lids would allow.

'Aung Cho? Am I dead or dreaming?'

She took his hand and held it with a gentle pressure.

'No, we are both alive. And your brothers too'. She gestured behind her. Skinny men in fatigues, some in tattered longyi (traditional dress) gathered round.

'The cyclone stopped us getting here sooner. We thought... we thought you might already be dead. The guards have gone. We found two of them dead in the jungle. Listen JamYang there's a treaty. We have to try and make peace now. Come, let us go home. Let us eat.'

The others joined her now, gently lifting

JamYang onto a bamboo stretcher.

'Zoya?' The single word stopped them in their tracks. The stretcher bearers turned their eyes to Aung Cho. She looked at the ground and then at JamYang, shaking her head slowly. 'We've had no word'.

JamYang motioned to the men to lower him. He tried to stand but fell back. 'Don't just stand there, help me up'.

Four pairs of arms scrabbled towards him, raising him by his arms. He stood and breathed in, trying not to close his eyes, trying not to think. 'We can eat when I get back'. JamYang took a canteen of water from one of the tribesmen and nodded his thanks. He limped slowly through the rubble and mess of building and jungle, Aung Cho calling his name behind him.

Who am I? Where am I? Why am I?

Inspired by the Canadian artist William Kurelek's painting of the same name

By Rebecca Nankivell

I look up with hands curled and outstretched simultaneously, illustrating the conundrum of my nomadic life. The Dutch landscape, maddeningly flat, spreads out north, south, east and west.

I raise my face to the Heavens for divine inspiration.

Which way to go?

Forwards, backwards, sideways, up or down?

Who knows the path, who cares which way I go?

'Lord God Almighty. Where am I?'

The dark earth silently slumbers beneath me. Doesn't look like God's in the ground tonight. There's no tomb - but what about the Cross? THE CROSS!

I go in search of Our Saviour on the cross. He has to be in Harlem. I got the message from Paul, and for sure Paul knows.

Light of the World: You stepped down into darkness. You saved me from the sins of the world. I gotta preach, gotta find the people who will listen. Get them to change their evil ways and turn their face to You.

'You are with me,' the light speaks, 'and I will never let you go'.

'Saviour of the World: who am I?'

But at that, the ground collapses beneath me and I struggle for air. My blanched, upturned face (still upturned) is blank.
'Jesus Christ: Why am I?'

I try one more question – where, who, why? - before the clods cover me and those wheres, whos and whys are silenced by oblivion.

The Rosary

By Bryan Rowe

It was just past mid-night on a still, bible black, Autumn night in a remote area of the countryside in Northern Ireland. At the end of a long overgrown track in the midst of a copse of fir trees, three men sat in an old ramshackle barn lit by an oil lamp hanging from an overhead beam. Leaning against some bales of hay, each man had a large haversack filled to bursting propped by their side. The thick mud clinging to their leather boots, evidence of their four mile trek across field and woodland escaping from the burglary they had carried out earlier that evening.

'Thank God we made it to Murphy's farm in one piece,' sighed Jago, as he tried to make himself more comfortable to ease the pain he felt in every limb of his body; he was certainly not used to so much exercise in one day.

'You're right, be Jasus,' replied Patrick. 'Every minute I feared the police would turn up, acting on a tip off on our raid on old Mallony's house.' He gave a loud snort, cleared his throat and proclaimed, 'Aye, and let's face it, our break in was a pure doddle, so it was; all his collectables just waiting to be collected.'

'Aye, including that bottle of whiskey you nicked from the sideboard,' joked Jago.

Each man took a generous swig from the bottle being passed around; for a moment the only sound came from the hiss of the oil lamp taking in the infused oil to feed its glowing flame, like the sound of air escaping from a deflating tyre.

Flynn, the third man, took another gulp of whiskey. 'Ah, that's a drop of good stuff so it is,' he said, as he wiped his mouth on the sleeve of his coat. A large rat appeared out of the darkness, stopped and looked inquisitively at him before scuttling off into the shadows.

'I wonder if rats like whiskey' queried Jago, as the bottle was passed to him.

'Don't suppose they've ever tried it,' replied Flynn.

'At least this bottle is 100% rat proof!' he laughed, as he tapped the side of the bottle and nursed it as though he was comforting a baby after its feed.

'Ach it's great that we can have this wee celebration here,' said Jago. 'We have enough booty between us to fund our local Ballylinnie cause for the next couple of years at least, so we have'.

Flynn glanced over to shovel leaning against the barn door.

'Ah tis a shame we have to bury all this stuff after all the trouble we've taken to get it,' he said. 'Still, it's only until all this blows over.'

He gave a loud yawn as he was handed the

bottle, took a swig , handed the bottle over to Patrick. Now bored by the constant prattle between them, Flynn fidgeted and pulled over his haversack closer to his side, unzipped it, fumbled around and took out a silver tea caddy. Making sure he had his back to the other two he pulled off the lid and inside found a small leather pouch containing a rosary. His face changed to a look of admiration.

Holy Mother of God, he whispered to himself. *It's beautiful.*

The familiar string of red beads had inset diamonds that reflected the light of the oil lamp. As a young boy, Flynn's father - a staunch member of the IRA - had been killed fighting in the Troubles. His mother, grief stricken, was unable to cope with her lively young son who was continually getting into bad company, so Flynn was sent to a Catholic boarding school. His mother regularly attended Mass and, in his mind's eye, Flynn could see her kneeling before the statute of the Holy Mother in their parlour at home, keeping count of her prayers as she gently moved the rosary beads between her fingers.

Jago stared across to Flynn.

'What have you got there?' he enquired.

'Just a silver tea caddy,' Flynn replied.

'Well,' said Jago, 'now we've finished the bottle we best be getting on and burying this stuff. Flynn, you take the shovel and start digging a hole at the back of that cart in the corner. Come morning we'll split up and go our separate ways; it will be much safer'.

Flynn pocketed the rosary. He knew exactly what he was going to do: he would take this precious find and, when he arrived home, he would give it to his mother as a gift - which to him would be a sign of the memory of his father's sacrifice to their cause, the cause they were still fighting.

Tu'chook Inlet

By Jane Marie MacGillivray

14th April 1978
Tu'chook Inlet,
Nilson Island,
Alaska

It was just after the "break-up" of ice on the Bering Sea inlet of Tu'chook, overlooking Cape Vancouver; Russia in front of us and U.S. Alaska behind us. I went out in my skiff, dodging floating icebergs and thick shards of beautifully fresh, jade-coloured sea ice, against the wishes of my aunt and uncle. It was imperative for me to see if the floating ice had backed-up and jammed, piling itself high-up on the shoreline, which might have damaged our clapboard and tin-roofed fish camp, along the coast at nearby Utqu'muit.

I started out when the sun was blazing, but, just over an hour into the journey, the weather changed dramatically to severe, gale force winds and a sudden hailstorm, just two miles or so short of our fish camp at Utqu'muit.

Pitch-blackened sky welded seamlessly together with the dark, metallic sea, until it morphed into one angry, panoramic backdrop, with neither definition nor the sight of popping, white, sea birds to guide the way around the coast.

Only just short of old Senka's, a tenth of a mile to go, is where I first turned the boat hard right, and made for the shore, as the waves of the Bering Sea broke over the sides, and began to fill its cavity. It smelled of raw, injured fish. Iced, sea-bed brine slapped my face hard, blistering every pore with alarm. My tongue grew wide at the back of my throat, unable to swallow my fright.

It was a little further in, fairly miniature and dilapidated, and I could barely, just see the rusted, tin roof through the weather, from the skiff. I landed on shore near to a shifting ice pack. I had nowhere else to stay, so I jumped out of my skiff, pulled it as far onto the shore as my adrenaline strength could manage, and bivouacked at Senka's fish camp.

Hunched forward, I drove into the BB-pelting hail, which raged sideways into me, and shot at the most defenceless parts of my body and skin. I walked onwards behind the small, tundra bluff and reached the door of Senka's camp. It was heavier than it looked, sagging to the right, and needed to be lifted-up with my left boot, while turning the metal latch carefully with my right hand, to avoid it snapping jaggedly in two, as the wood had rotted and the corroded hinges were missing a couple of screws. It only partially opened, and I slickly squeezed myself into Senka's domain. It was small, maybe even 8' X 10' feet. There was enough room for a place to sleep, a sideboard made of flotsam with three shelves, a corner stove made from a small, metal oil drum with a pipe straight out the roof, and the floor covered in a pile of old fishing nets needing mended.

It was a respected place, even though Senka had long-died over a decade ago. He had been a gifted shaman, and everyone for miles still respected his camp, letting nature take it back into the ground.

Senka had been a locally known explorer, gifted at identifying and mapping fresh fishing grounds around the Bering Sea area nearer to his village of Tu'chook Inlet. It was a role of some enormity, as it kept his people furnished with food aplenty; the bounty of the sea. No one ever underestimated Senka's innate talent for finding schools of herring fish, aganaqsayaks, halibut, bream, salmon, and creatures that lurked in the dark, icy depths of the Bering Sea. He was highly esteemed and his Yu'pik Nation depended on the diversity of his mapping skills to direct the village men to abundant fishing grounds. It was almost biblical, and Senka was well-respected as he had an incredible memory for markers at sea.

As I sat in my wet oilskins for a couple of hours recovering, sitting on a small hillock of maritime debris, ragged ends of rope, oval floats and manky, tattered fishing nets; my eyes probed the dank corner to my left, where I saw the identifiable form of what looked as if it promised food, or at least something flavoured to add to my flask. I scrambled over and blindly felt the distinct shape of a coffee can, which I lifted excitedly, for the weighty content, had already brewed the vision of a steaming cup of joe, even before I lifted the lid. Instead, I was taken aback staring stunned at the contents, which usurped my thirst and riveted all my thoughts into a quango of inquisitiveness.

This is the Amicorum Album I found in a rusting 5lb. coffee can, inside the low ceiling lean-to of Senka Ivanoff's fish camp. It appeared to be a diary of a journey taken, with seen objects and landscapes meticulously hand-sketched, and a couple of old photographs, acquired along the way. There was also, a dented snuff box, and two small bundles, each as big as my fist, wrapped in a swaddling of dried seal gut, together with another elongated item in a stiff, leather pouch.

My right hand held poised, shrewdly deciding upon which item to select. Which to choose first?

Should I really be doing this; unravelling Senka's private property? What would my people think of this? Maybe, I shouldn't. I'm not even old enough to have gained respect from the Yu'pik Nation, or *The Real People* as we were known, when translated into the language of the Gasaks. I would have to be somewhere around eighty-nine to one hundred and ten years old for that privilege. I've been bad. I'm a bad listener at school, too. I'm always doing clumsy stuff, and getting into trouble.

"Hm."

I'm young and stupid enough to have been caught-out in a storm, against my relative's wishes.

What my aunt and uncle must have thought, with the adverse weather conditions, and without news? They'd probably have lowered themselves to their knees with anxious prayers for my safe return. They must have been in a dire way with the fear that comes with a thud in your gut telling you that your caregiver and entire pension may have gone for good.

I arrived today, on a Tuesday, and might need to stay for a few hours, or maybe another day or two, before the weather quells. It might be a while, and I'm just bored.

I started to unravel the lumps placed on fish nets before me, and begun the secret journey into Senka's history and his secret stuff.

Starting with the larger of the two lumps; I picked at the grimy husk to get at a tag-end of the seal gut wrapping. It was oozing with rancid oil, sticky and smelled like the butt-end of a garbage bin. It started to unpeel, until I came to the centre of it, which was just a lump of old, waxy walrus blubber.

What was Senka thinking? Was it leftovers of food, which he stowed on a past journey, then brought it home, and forgot about it? He *was* old and by himself. Who knows?

I squeezed its odd, waxy shape, then, pinched it hard. There was something solid in the middle of the rotten blubber. I picked away at it, as it really stunk and I didn't want the whole fermented piece to go down my sleeve by accident. The first glint appeared.

"Huh?"

Small, steady breaths arrested the rankling stink. I didn't smell a thing after that. Only, my eyes doubled in size and the reflex of it lit a fuse of such proportion, that my mind's intellectual strongbox finally flung, wide-open, as if by fission. My attention was as focussed as laser precision.

That first item was fairly untarnished and drew me in immediately. It appeared to be a golden amulet, with a caged golden nugget as a sceptre at its peak, crowning two golden bees at either side, and dangling three amber pieces, framed in gold beneath them. When inspected carefully, there were minute clumps of fine baby hair with roots, imbedded in each amber cell. The back of the amulet had an engraving with a crown, a Russian Orthodox cross and a letter "R."

It wasn't a large piece, which fitted neatly across my two fingers, and had a fine pin at the back. I examined it close to my face, and studied its ornate embellishment. I had seen those crosses before in many of the Russian Orthodox villages, up and down the Yukon and Kuskokwim River Delta. I stuck the amulet brooch onto my sleeve, and kept it in sight.

This time, there was no further hesitation, when I reached for the second lump. It was a bit heavier than the first one, but, I picked away at the wrap delicately, so as not to damage the treasure inside. When I split the fetid, blubber in half, out slipped a triangular stone with a large hole drilled in the centre of it. My eyebrows along with the tone, lowered together in disappointment.

The shaped stone was polished alabaster, the triangular corners smoothed; almost rounded. It felt good in my hand. I turned it over and over, flipped it from corner to corner, and stuck every one of my fingers on my left hand through the hole in the centre. It was as smooth as Aunties' face, but, what was it for? Fishing weight, maybe? I placed it close to my eye and viewed the interior of the hut through the hole in the stone, framing all that came into view. It helped to focus.

I placed it on my packsack, lying beside me on the nets. It was a curio of sorts, and a dozen questions flit through my head of its use. It must have had a practical application.

Back into the can went my hand to retrieve the dented snuff tin, and bring it out into the open. I rattled it near to my right ear, and it resounded in harmonic clanks. It unsnapped easily enough, considering that it was a bit rusty on the top and sides.

The contents were simple enough for any fisherman; with the remnants of actual snuff, various-sized fish hooks and small weights, a button, coins with holes in them, a small key, a bullet and a couple of needles. Not too exciting, but, I tried a pinch of the stale snuff inside my bottom lip.

The coffee can was turned upside down, with the final item having fallen onto my lap. I slid the lengthy object out of the crumbling leather pouch and into the bowl of my hands.

It was a folded, measuring device, hand-carved out of the flat ribs of a walrus, with perfectly rounded joins or pins made of ivory at the end of each rib. It was engineered meticulously, slickly folding and reopening with ease.

The folding stick had demarcations of measurements engraved along the length of the margin on one side, and stars and constellations depicted on the opposite margin of the same side. It was reversed on the other side of the measuring stick, and etched with the four seasons; Winter was the longest by far. The celestial bodies and star constellations which I recognized; Venus, the North Star, Big Dipper, the Seven Sisters, Cassiopeia, and then, many others unknown to me, were beautifully scrimshawed onto the surface of the ribs.

Senka must have kept his bearings at Sea with the use of his measuring device, charting the stars in their position on various voyages, across the seasons, and then safely returning home to Tu'chook Inlet.

My respect for Senka had begun to escalate, when I closely studied his simply-hewn, yet highly calibrated masterpiece of design. It was minimalist in design, but completely genius in its precision and application.

I carefully placed it next to the triangular stone on my packsack nearby.

There was a filthy cardboard box tied and knotted with dried seal gut, planted just underneath the can, which was displaced, and in appearance, looked as if they went together. The gut wrapping demarked rancid, sticky seal oil which had seeped onto the cover of the box, indicating that a long stretch of time had elapsed since last the box was opened.

Meanwhile, the force of the gale thumped heavily at the clapboard walls and lean-to ceiling. Dried sea grass and dust mortar spiralled through the slats in quiet puffs. My spine shuddered on impulse; and yet I was entirely transfixed on the grubby box, and only faintly recognized the encrypted warning of hypothermia that came with lashings of hailstones on the corrugated tin roof above. I was cold.

I reached low for the box off the shelf, but only the lid came away in my hand, the bottom was a disintegrated mess underneath. There were filthy down feathers inside, and the wings of an Arctic Tern, glued together by the gumminess of the oil. They camouflaged a fair-sized lump lying on its side, half-implanted in the cavity of the decayed bird, which the tundra shrews had eaten-away into a freeze-dried wafer.

The smell was a bit ripe and stank of a fusty, flea-ridden, animal skin. I poked at it with my flask. It was firm. With an extra nudge, the weight of it all dropped the bottom shelf into a hole in the floor beneath it. Nothing else moved, not even the lump.

My pulse recovered quickly after a couple of deep breaths, when I reassured myself that the demon lump was well and truly dead. I grabbed it this time with both, gloved hands, and brought the whole mess close to my gut.

"What is that? *Cauga?*"

I pulled small handfuls of the gooey down and rank hide off the object. It was rectangular, thick and not as heavy as it looked. When it was brushed-off, I started to unwind the parched seal gut which had protected it. There was about seven feet of it, almost as translucent as papyrus paper, with the seal oil, which had seeped into it over time, and now smelled of the fresh open sea. There it was, as pristine as a birthday gift, sitting on my lap, the unwound wrappings of dried gut paper at my feet. A book. An ancient book bound in spotted seal skin velum, with gold leaf written embellishments on the spine and cover; Cyrillic. Russian Cyrillic.

Throwing my gloves off, I carefully opened the front cover and saw writing-- backwards written letters and symbols. I knew that it was Russian Cyrillic writing, a piece of art with arrows and diagrams to scale, a pièce de résistance, so minute was the detailed drawing that it drew me into a dreamy fairyland of majestic beauty.

A thickness of pages was turned, to reveal

a tin box, die-cut and implanted into the depth of the book itself; a wee dull, zinc tin within a treasured book of fascinating feathered drawings, in minute, hatched strokes, of something diminutive in its construction.

I wedged out the tin, and it plopped out easily onto my lap. I shook it a little, but couldn't open it. There was an intricate latch with a small keyhole underneath it. I just couldn't get it open, as hard as I tried. I poked at it with a sliver of wood, and thought about smashing it open with the triangular stone, yet, something inside of my gut told me to try another way. I remembered the little key inside of the snuff box, and thought that I would give it a try.

I spat the snuff out into a corner of the room, and reached for the small tin. My fingers fished-out the diminutive key and I closed the tin momentarily, as I was none too convinced that it was the right fit.

It dropped onto the net.

Where was it?

Rubbing my hand over the bobbly surface of the net, I caught the wee key between my fingers, and fumbled it into the tiny keyhole of the dull zinc box without much emotional fanfare.

It was turned, and clicked open. I lifted the lid and caught the familiar aroma and sight of the waxy, walrus blubber and dried seal gut encasement inside. Once again, I painstakingly peeled the roughage back, with cold, stiffened fingers, and panted frosty breaths. Then, everything just stopped.

A lustrous sparkle illuminated a chink in its fetid blubber encasement. And with disbelief at its ornate promise, I extracted a jewelled egg of exquisite haute design and beauty.

I now had a picture in my mind of what I needed to do. Senka was speaking to me through this truth.

It was with deliberate care that I repackaged the newfound treasures belonging to Senka, and with ceremony placed them all on the top shelf of his flotsam sideboard.

I loosened the door at the front of the small, oil drum stove with a wee kick, and opened it. All of the rank, stinking walrus and seal gut encasements and wrappings went in, and I lit it instantly with a lighter from my packsack. It was freezing in the fish camp.

I took a good few gulps of chai from my flask, grabbed the smooth, triangular stone from the shelf, laid down, and covered myself up with some of the old nets needing mended.

The triangular stone felt good repositioned in my hand. I turned it over and over, flipped it from corner to corner. It made me focus in thought. Was it a contemplation stone? I could picture Senka, in my mind's eye, with his face to the night sky, measuring distances between stars, and calibrating his exacting journey, a mere fleck on the imperious Bering Sea, pointing his boat in the direction of home at Tu'chook Inlet, and his people; the

Real People; the people, who depended on their good shaman, Senka, for direction to the fishing and hunting grounds of abundance.

Senka was a lion-hearted leader. He was at home with his sea challenges and adventures; he mapped and explored for his people, and problem-solved with his own superior intellect. He was a man of practical knowledge, who invented and used his primitive-looking tools and methods and the ancient stars as guiding friends, when in isolation on the dark Bering Sea of Western Alaska.

It had become warm in Senka's fish camp, and my eyes became heavy, but my mind was illuminated. The triangular stone clutched in my palm.

The folded measuring tool and stone needed more research, along with Senka's carefully illustrated Amicorum Album as a reference, which would be of great cultural interest to our people. It was a charter of life-long exploration and edification.

The village was in desperate need of a new radio system for emergencies, supplies and incoming planes; and equally important was the need of a film recorder and new video camera to record meetings with outside companies and the government, in order not to taken for granted or cheated.

Conservation of our sea beds and fishing grounds was paramount to us, and we needed strong representation to ensure there'd be no further oil speculation.

And now at last, we had the tools to fight them. At auction, the gold amulet brooch and the Faberge egg would see to our financial concerns for a lengthy time to come. Senka, our good shaman, had once again saved his people.

I closed my eyes and slept, and dreamt of my skiff out on the Bering Sea sailing in the direction of fresh adventure. I held the measuring tool high above my head and raised my bare face toward the night sky, using the celestial coordinates, which Senka had exacted with his markings. The light of countless Northern stars shimmered across the great night sky like beloved ancestors blessing my journey.

A Cornish Evening

By Pam Rowe

The stage is set ready for the players. This unusual stage was part of an amphitheatre carved out of rock by the sea in Cornwall. It was used regularly through the summer, with an audience most nights. The evening would start with the excited people arriving and, as the seats filled up, the atmosphere and hum of voices would gradually build up to a crescendo so it was difficult to identify any individual conversation.

Louise was in her dressing room, ready to meet her leading man on stage in a few minutes. She had a lot of nerves and hoped she would not get stage fright and forget her words, as this was the first time she had performed Romeo and Juliet.

Theatre had been a love of hers since childhood,and she entered RADA at age eighteen. It had been her ambition since childhood, but the competition to enter RADA was great. Now, having completed her course, she was in Rep and travelled most of Britain touring different theatres. She had found this very rewarding as she could study several cultures and dialects along the way.

Her leading man and Louise had

become very close during the tour and she was hoping the relationship would develop over the next year or two, but in the meantime to-night had to be dealt with. She finalised her make-up, dressed and was ready for her entrance.

Her leading man arrived at the dressing room door and asked:

'Are you ready Louise? Can I come in?'

''Yes come in, Mario. I'm ready.'

He entered, and was taken in by her beauty as he always was. He felt he was falling in love with this girl but was afraid to tell her, hoped with this special performance of Romeo and Juliet he would at last come clean on his feelings.

They made their way together to the wings of the stage. The night was clear and the sea sparkling under the moonlight. The atmosphere hushed in anticipation of the oncoming event. They both entered the stage and played the performance of their lives, putting all their pent up emotions into it. It concluded, and the audience went mad and stood up clapping and cheering. At least it had been a success. The couple and the rest of the cast came on to the stage for an encore.

At last they all went back stage.

There was a party in the moonlight on the beach to follow. All sitting around a fire made from driftwood found on the beach, they laughed and joked and reminisced over the earlier events and hoped there would be an opportunity to return to this unusual setting.

At the end of the evening, Mario decided to tell Louise how he felt because he found this place was so magical and he wanted the explanation of his affections to be remembered in this gorgeous spot and - if Louise felt the same way - one day they could return together as husband and wife to reminisce on this night of enchantment that was so new to him.

She's Booked!

By Josephine S. J. Sumner

We had come with great expectations to the island that summer many years ago. I was fifteen at the time, neither one or the other, a girl nor a woman – an awkward, giggly, blushing age.

It rained non-stop, lashing wind and rain. My sister and myself got fed up in the end, almost climbing the walls with frustration. The owner of the hotel where we were staying must have realised, perhaps we'd been bickering a bit too loudly.

Anyway, she came to us and said, 'There's a library at the back of the hotel still intact from when it was a private house owned by the McCleods. Shall I show you?'.

'Okay,' we said, not too enthusiastically - but anything to alleviate the boredom.

We were led to a beautiful wood-panelled room with shelves of books from floor to ceiling.

'Here we are. Feel free to borrow and read any you like, as long as you put them back.'

With that she left us.

'Wow!' I said. 'It would take years to read all these.'

'I wouldn't want to. Look at this: *Household Tips of the 17th Century.* Totally obsolete.'

'There are good crumbs of advice, sometimes, amongst the chaff.'

'Spare me, sis. I'm going to get comfy on this chair by the window and snooze.'

I walked around, looking at random books: *The History of Scotland, 'Naval History, Kings and Queens.*

They all seemed so dry.

Then I saw this section in a dark corner: *The Clan McCleod.* I didn't know much about it, did I want to learn? Next to *The Clan McLeod* books was an old, leather-bound book without any title. I brushed the dust off and opened it at a random page: *How to have men fascinated by you,* it said. I read the page and re-read it. Information I could use in the future. It said it was important to be yourself. That's obvious isn't it? Then I thought of eighteen year old Penny Waites who lived next door to us at home. She'd been going off to watch the local football team.

'Do you like football?' I asked.

'Not really, but it keeps Tony happy.'

What a waste of her time, was she being herself?

Not really.

Couldn't they have done something they both liked in their precious spare time?

There was some faint writing at the

bottom of the page: *Marry in haste, repent at leisure.*

Obviously that meant you had to get to know someone before you took the plunge. Had the writer of that missive fascinated a man too quickly and it had all gone pear-shaped? How long did you fascinate a man for until you knew he was *The One*?

Mrs. Bradley, up the road, had been married three times. Did she think it was *The One* three times? When did *The One* not become *The One* anymore?

I feel as if I've got an awful lot to learn.

What else does it say?

Keep a part of yourself secret - that adds to the mystery. Your lover senses this and respects you for it.

But what part do you keep secret? Well, farting and belching perhaps, unless they slip out, and your monthlies I supposed. The fact that I hate being enclosed, am frightened by small spaces and feel claustrophobic. Surely he would find that out?

There's more writing in the margin.

Tried that, was still slaughtered.

Oh!

Maybe she didn't keep enough secret.

What is enough? Where is the yardstick?

I would feel embarrassed asking mum.

She would probably say I'd got plenty of time ahead for that sort of thing.

Anyway, she's always working on her computer. She's doing it now, up in her hotel bedroom. Dad stayed in Inverness.

Surely if you prepare you are less likely to make mistakes.

I will definitely borrow this book.

Barnabus and the Boss's Wife

By Kenneth Blyth

Barnabus sitting in his office sipping tea
Giles barges through the door looking like
a startled deer in headlights

Giles: We're in big trouble.

Barnabus: Oh *(withdrawn)*

Giles: It's quite important, Sir. You may wish to take care of this personally.

Barnabus: Have we lost money? Did John break the coffee machine again?

Giles: No but...

Barnabus: Is somebody injured?

Giles: No

Barnabus: Well...

Giles: Sir, the boss's wife. She's here.

Barnabus: Ah...

Barnabus hastily puts down his cup turns around opens the window and looks down at the ground

Barnabus: Giles, how far down do you think?

Giles: Em...about fifty meters, Sir.

Barnabus: Damn! We need curtains, shoe laces, anything. I refuse to be in the same building as that woman. Why isn't the Boss taking care of her?

Giles: He's detained.

Barnabus: I'm sure he is, the dirt under his nails requires a great deal of attention.

Barnabus franticly walks around his desk

Barnabus: So, Giles what do we do? We are trapped. The enemy has us surrounded and there's no means of escape

Giles: Surrender?

Barnabus: Never! Not to her! Where is she now?

Giles: Reception sir.

Barnabus pauses and looks at Giles in the chair

Barnabus: Still time. Get John to stall her

Giles: Sir?

Barnabus: Just do I;, have him talk about his stamp collection

Giles: He doesn't have one.

Barnabus: Whatever then. The fire escape on this floor is nearby. We might just have a chance if John is convincing enough

Giles: Right away sir.

Barnabus and Giles walk out the office into the corridor and head towards the fire escape, making sure no one can see them. Giles reaches for his mobile and dials John

Giles: Hello John, yes fine, and you? Excellent. Listen, I need a favour. The Boss's wife, yes, you met her last year. She commented on your shirt and non-matching trousers. You commented on her shoes she didn't speak to you again after. Well, she's here and heading for Barnabus. We need you to keep her away while he prepares his office, get some tea going. You know how it is...Ah good man

Giles: It's done

Barnabus: We've lost a brave man today

They approach the fire exit immediately greeted by the harsh weather and begin claiming own

Barnabus: We're been tested today, Giles. But this is better than the alternative. Down these stairs, to the car, and were home free

The two men climb down to the next floor. Their colleagues can see them through their windows

Barnabus: Damn it! Don't these people have work to do?

They continue to climb down to the first floor. Giles glances through the window and immediately ducks

Giles: Gets down Sir!

Barnabus: Why?

He looks through the window, seeing John and the Wife talking, and ducks

Both men are now hiding under the window sill

Barnabus: Oh!

Barnabus: If she sees us now were done for. Giles, can you peek a look? See where they're going?

Giles peeks over the window sill, doing his best too look inconspicuous

He observes John doing his best to keep her occupied

Going by the blank look on her face it wasn't working

Giles: I think John is losing his battle Sir he's faltering.

Barnabus: How long?

Giles: A minute at most, before he surrenders

Barnabus: Let's go then

They proceed to the bottom

Giles takes one last quick look thought the window

He sees the Wife going up the stairs to Barnabus's office

Giles: Quickly, Sir! Before she reaches your window!

Barnabus: Faster man! The car is just there!

They sprint to the car and get in

Barnabus's face washes over with relief

Barnabus: We've done it!

He starts the car and drives off

He laughs

Then Giles' phone rings

Giles: Hello? Ah John. Sorry we had to dash, emm... Barnnabus had to...

He hangs up

Barnabus looks at him, eyebrow raised

Giles: Tunnel Sir.

After a short drive Barnabus and Giles pull over to a nearby café to celebrate their victory

The clink drinks at their table

Barnabus: Magnificent   work   today,

Giles. Without you I'd be stuck there with her, wishing for a quick death

Giles: No problem, Sir. Might be worth avoiding the Boss. He will not be pleased once she's had her way with him.

Barnabus: I'll win him over.

The two men sit

A car pulls up outside the café

The boss and his Wife exit the car

Giles: Sir!

Barnabus: Giles, it's been a pleasure knowing you

Giles: Likewise, Sir.

Before Barnabus can respond, the couple walk in

The wife notices Barnabus immediately

Wife: Barney, you old dog! Where have you been?

The two men sit, accepting their fate.

The Abyss

By Bryan Rowe

It was starting to snow as Marcel arrived at the Jungle. For the past twelve months, as a member of the French Police, he had been responsible for policing the refugee camp two miles outside Calais- now famously known as The Jungle. He gave a heavy sigh as he walked over the rough frozen ground towards a group of his colleagues who were waiting at the main police checkpoint to receive their orders for the duties of the day. His stride was measured, mechanical but with the confidence of a Robo-Cop. Dressed in protective clothing, complete with helmet and visor, the anonymity of his appearance hid his feelings about the demanding task he faced each day.

Marcel viewed the whole ongoing situation with complete contempt, the police were expected to achieve the impossible. The three thousand refugees encamped within the vast complex of makeshift shacks and tents had grown more and more restless, frustrated and belligerent. Groups of men were continually attacking lorry drivers to gain access to their vehicles in their bid for freedom. More new refugees arrived each day to get lost in the seething mass of foreign bodies confined within the Jungle. Marcel saw the scene that faced him each day as an abyss, a black hole with no ending. He had to obey orders to keep control, yet who controlled the daily exodus from the many far eastern countries the refugees were fleeing from?

He arrived at the main checkpoint where the others were awaiting expectantly for the arrival of Sergeant Boulez, the Chief Officer for their section. The air was clouded with smoke from the many fires people had lit to cook their food and keep warm. A group of children were using a large frozen puddle as a skating rink, laughing as they skidded on the ice, oblivious of the problems facing the police that day. A middle aged man and woman were distributing pots of yoghurt from the back of a van. A queue was forming at a tent where mobile phones could be charged and sim cards purchased. Marcel hated the continual intrusion of I Phone cameras and TV reporters. It was as if everyone needed to capture each movement made by the police to identify which factor was out of line.

Marcel turned to his friend Pierre who was stamping his feet on the ground to keep warm.

'To-day is going to be a complete nightmare,' Pierre complained. 'Whatever were the courts in Lille thinking about when they gave our government the go-ahead to evict a thousand of these people from the camp? Where the hell are they supposed to go'.

'Don't worry, mon Pierre,' replied Marcel. 'They certainly won't evaporate. They'll just move back into the remaining part of the camp, or set up temporary shelters along the shore - which will mean more surveillance for us. It's the women and kids who will really suffer from all this.'

A police car suddenly appeared, shuddered to a halt, from which Sergeant Boulez and two other officers alighted. Boulez stood in front of the assembled group - a tall heavily built man who always reminded Marcel of General De Gaulle.

'This morning your job is to allow access for our men clearing the south side of the camp, so that they can load the lorries with all the debris and rubbish safely. Already two of our men have been injured by bricks and stones being thrown at them.'

When Marcel and his contingent arrived at the scene, they were greeted by a crowd of angry men and youths chanting and waving their arms in protest at the intrusion as police tore down the ugly structures of the makeshift shacks and loaded the rubbish onto the lorries.

Amidst all the ensuing chaos, as Marcel pushed a group of angry onlookers to the side, he came across a young Asian woman sitting on a box having her arm bandaged by a Red Cross worker. He was immediately struck by her exquisite looks, a real eye-catcher, a woman who would stand out in a crowded room. Dressed in a green woollen jumper and faded torn blue jeans, her piercing blue eyes fixed directly on

Marcel.

Her tearful expression was one of complete despair.

'What is happening?' she asked. 'You are destroying the only shelter we have. I left Afghanistan after losing my husband and young son. My home was also destroyed after an attack on our village by the Taliban. I walked for months to get this far and, even then, when I arrived here in France those terrorists had just carried out that terrible massacre in Paris, and we were harassed by people who saw us as the enemy. I only wish this frozen earth would open up and swallow me.'

Marcel looked at the Red Cross worker, raised his head, shrugged his shoulders and walked away.

The young woman remained motionless as she watched the policeman walk away to face the angry mob. She was sick of the indifference of the life she had led over the past few months: the indifference of the Authorities, who told her she would have to wait nine months for her application for asylum to be considered. She just couldn't get away from war, death and loss, and had ended up in this awful place.

Now she was being thrown out into the abyss.

As Marcel drove home to his flat in the centre of Calais, at the end of his shift, on his car radio a news reader reported on the action the police had taken that day to start to clear a thousand refugees from The Jungle. A politician blathered on about the need for Britain to take more responsibility over the refugee problem, and stated a camp should be set up in Dover.

The face of the young woman he'd met that morning was still indelibly etched in his mind's eye.

You will just have to move to another abyss, he said to himself.

As the traffic lights ahead changed to red, Marcel slowed down to take his place in the line of stationary cars. A crowd of men and women were standing at the side of the road and suddenly the woman in the green jumper appeared, ran out to the side of his car and banged her fist on its bonnet. Looking at Marcel she turned and pointed to the group of onlookers, and shouted:

'All this has got to stop! Where are we supposed to go now you have moved us out?'

For what seemed like minutes, Marcel and the woman continued to stare at each other transfixed, mutually sharing the frustrations of their places in the ongoing enigma. The lights turned to green and a honk on the horn from the driver behind him prompted Marcel to get into gear and drive away.

Throughout his journey home, it dawned on him again that the events of the day had demonstrated how futile the role of the police had become.

There would be no end to the number of refugees flooding into France and - with the added problem of terrorism - he knew his job as a policeman would never be the same again.

The Mandarin, the Hawk and the Fritillary

By Becky Nankivell

'It's your lead', Sam said as he finished dealing the cards. Pete, the hawker, had all spades bar one so knew he was onto a winner.

'Spades,' he said, calling out trumps. *Let's finish this hand and get out,* he was thinking - not that he was indoors, for the three friends played cards each night on low wooden stools outside the stone one storey houses with their flat, lead roofs where the mandarin peels dried out in the sun.

Pete led with his only heart, and Jim won that hand. Jim - known as Jim da Rin, after his trade of hawking mandarin skins from village to town – next slapped down a seven of spades while watching a purple-bodied dragonfly gracefully skim the village pond. Not noticing Sam's disappointment when Pete beat his king with an ace, Pete next leading absentmindedly with an ace of clubs. He too wanted to get a move on before the rains came. It was his habit to check all the pithy mandarin rinds after their card game and choose the driest to load onto the wooden racks and baskets of his bicycle.

Sam was the only one who took the game

seriously. Stuck with a gammy leg and an inky heart that prevented him from the heights Pete got to with his hawk, or the breadths Jim pedaled to with his trade, Sam knew the village in its manifold forms. He could recognize the voices of folk on the outskirts, knew when there were strangers approaching, could tell which family it was cooking their garlic rice.

Sam never missed a smidgeon, but could be taken for a ride when it came to the latest trade talk. Jim was your guy in that department.

'Jim, you pillock,' Sam chided, 'Pete played the ace. Its his lead."

Jim didn't care, just followed Pete's spade and causally won the hand, Pete turning with disgust to check on his hooded hawk who was protesting that it was time to hunt.

Sam sighed. Why did no one take their game to heart anymore? He wanted the village to stay as it was, but times were changing. He was shocked to find that even his mind was straying from the game tonight, Pete having to nudge him into playing the next card.

All things bright and beautiful,
All creatures great and small...

The hymn's refrain was echoing around Sam's head as he tried to find his heart.

How do I know I've got a heart?

The thought in his mind before he could stop it, listening to the beating beneath his skin.

All things wise and wonderful,
The Lord God made them all.

The refrain grew louder, and Sam

wondered why he'd never returned to the land of his birth. He'd grown up on a farm in Devon, helped his dad and brothers to lamb and calve. He'd cried the first time he'd seen the slithering calf slip out from its mother, it's blue cord like a fifth slippery leg wobbly and unsure. He'd taken the sound of the skylark for granted, and had himself larked in the wide open spaces, seeing the creatures of the burrow - hares, weasels and rabbits - dashing across the fields. The tall-hedged lanes had held him in, until one day he found himself on the other side of the hemisphere, bewildered as to how he'd arrived, abandoned by his beloved family, needing to forget the days of his youth in order to survive.

Why am I thinking of them now?

Jim had given up, laying down his cards.

But Jim had already darted up onto the blue-gray roof and began sifting his rinds, filling his baskets, breathing in the sweet scent of the sun-dried fruit skins, loading the baskets onto his bike, patiently covering the wooden planks of his trailer until it resembled a milky orange sky, before he lugged an old tarp over the fruit peels. Then he lay down beside his cart and went to sleep, just like that. He needed it if he was to be ready for his predawn start, that would have him ride in a fifty mile radius shouting all day:

Come and get your quality peels!
This mandarin the best in Gordoia!
Come on doctors, heal your patients –
Only the best for your herbal preparation!

Come flavour your candy!
Only the best from Jim da Rin.

Pete left soon after Jim had bedded down, hawking glove already on his hand, taking Jinkouwei to the edge of the field and out onto the mud track that led up to the land where he could hunt. On his way, he heard the sound of a pipe breaking through his thoughts, and then a drum beat. Jinkouwei, unhooded, was flying free, doing his usual circling. Twenty eight years they'd been together, Pete and his hawk, and never once had Jinkouwei left Pete in all that time.

The music stopped as the rain began, but from his high vantage point Pete could see the men approaching his village. He could see Jim's sleeping form by his cart. Jim had the knack of being able to sleep anywhere and through anything. When his bike wasn't loaded the racks made a comfortable bed, but when they were full - like tonight - he didn't mind the earth as his resting spot.

Pete whistled, but Jinkouwei was out of sight. Not unusual, but Pete shivered as the rain trickled down his neck, his thin t-shirt clinging to his back.

Down in the village, Sam went inside when the rain came. He was too old, and his leg hurt. It took a while to hobble across his room to the side where his box-bed lay, and carefully lay down.

All things bright and beautiful.

He thought of the musicians who had just arrived in the village.

He thought of Pete up there in the mountain with his hawk.

He thought of Jim lying next to his precious mandarin peels, the same tarpaulin covering them both.

Everything was changing.

He eventually slept, and then he dreamt: saw a fritillary skimming the village pond. It was all so familiar, and he could smell the stale water as the fritillary flew by. And then suddenly – as is the way with dreams - he was in the pond with water, right up to his neck. The water was rising, and the stink was overwhelming.

He was going to drown, or die from a bad smell.

Of that he was convinced.

Sam still seated nursing his wounds having lost not only another game but the shame of Pete and Jim abandoning it and not even caring his ears perked up. A melodious piping rising in volume wafted closer to the village. Then a drum beat. How could Jim sleep through this? Sam thought.

Broken Shell – a novel

By Kenneth Blyth

Set up

Earth 3998AD

Humans achieved interstellar travel around 2300AD with the creation of the Ribbon Drive; expanding to the stars made massive advances in technology, created and lost an empire after several long bloody civil wars. Over the course of several bombardments Earth was left uninhabitable, the surviving population fleeing to six giant orbital stations (old defence platforms) around the planet. Earth is cut off from its colonies and empire, leaving it in centuries' long isolation, technology beginning to regress in this weakened state. The stations' ancestors set up giant terraforming machines to restore the planet, their long work progressing at a slow rate, while the planet continues to be a lifeless rock.

Mars

Mars is inhabited by a large population, bigger than all the other stations combined; another victim of bombardment, the population exist in a post-apocalyptic society with little contact with the other stations. The rich, and those who've forced their way in, live in large environmental domes were they live a life of relative comfort and safety. The rest of the population have to live in small sealed shanty towns scattered around the domes making oxygen, food and water precious resources. Any ship that lands or is shot down on Mars outside the domes is immediately stripped of parts and used to construct shelters and maintain what little technology is left. There are few exceptions to this rule, but smugglers - or anyone who would bring in advanced technology and illegal substances - are spared. The domes' population also reward those that bring in high value goods and will protect ships escorting them to landing pads within the giant structures.

Despite the risks, some people from the stations attempt to risk the journey, seeing it as an escape from their own station's oppressive lifestyle and claustrophobic confines. With nothing left on Earth, Mars is the best place to put their feet on the ground. As such, the stations use propaganda and harsh travel restrictions to keep their citizens in line, the populations on the stations so small that everyone has to contribute to the stations' survival, where any significant loss of population could be devastating.

Stations

Floating orbital cities around earth contain the last of earth's population, flora and fauna. All except Hadrian are in disrepair, as the knowledge and skill to maintain the systems have been lost.

Each has its own methods of government and defence.

Hadrian

Largest of the six, and the only station to be fully operational and thus considered a near impenetrable fortress

Nerva

Second largest Station, trading hub, large port.

Houses a small but elite defence force.

Society divided into castes led by The Hegemony.

Juno

Home of The Order of Nightingales, their aim to reclaim lost knowledge and technology in an attempt to reunify humanity peacefully.

But will fiercely defend itself if attacked.

It has a large force of AI controlled ships

Vulcan

Went silent two centuries ago.

Any force investigating is shot down by the station's defence grid.

Those that make it in are never heard from again.

Even The Huntresses give it a wide birth

Diana
Home of The Huntresses.

The smallest and deadliest of the remaining stations.

Population trained from birth how to fight.

It has been invaded several times in the past by the bigger stations.

Augustus
Destroyed by a civil war.

The rulers of the station previously controlled the populace with an iron fist, eventually leading to a bloody coup that resulted in massive damage to the station, and its eventual destruction.

Debris from the station is considered a traffic risk to passing ships.

The Action
Synopsis

The story tells the adventures of Captain Malcom and his crew on the Starship Mab, a Frigate of Station Nerva. While on patrol the Mab is ordered to intercept the cargo ship Helides. The crew of the Helides are afflicted by some strange contagion; despite the Helides captain's attempt to warn Malcom it is too late and the Helides crew transform into feral lupine monsters. Malcom and crew defeat the creatures and search the Helides for any clues. One crewman finds a mysterious cube in the captain's quarters and is ordered to take it back to the Mab for study.

The cube is revealed to be from Vulcan - Nerva's sister station. Malcom decides to head back to Nerva to keep the cube safe and study it, however on the journey back they are attacked by an unknown ship. During the fire fight, a boarding party from the enemy ship gets onto the Mab. Security Officer Davidson and a security team intercept the boarding party. A solitary attacker knocks out the security team; the Mab damages the enemy enough to halt the attach briefly and Davidson takes her chance. As the firefight ensues, the cube glows and merges with Davidson, giving her the strength to defeat the Avatar, after which the cube's energy dissipates, the Avatar disappears and Davidson is left on the ground unconscious.

The Mab limp's home to Nerva and is put in for extensive repairs.

Malcom meets Admiral Smith and reports the situation. Smith tells Malcom that the Mab will take some time before she is repaired, and that the crew and Malcom are stuck on Nerva for the time being.

Malcom visits Munro at the University – Munro is trying to figure out the writing on the cube. After some time, he translates some of the writing and learns that the cube is a centuries' old repository of knowledge designed by scientists on Vulcan as a means of storing the great thinkers and citizens of the station. However, others on Vulcan discovered the technology and fought over it, and soon the "wrong minds" were being uploaded. After this, a defence mechanism was put in place by The Orthographik Order to prevent unwanted usage, keep the "wrong minds" out and the knowledge safe. Over time, the sheer amounts of minds gave the cube a form of self-awareness.

Meanwhile Green is kidnapped from a bar and is put in a cell with a young blind women names Roberta. After a short time, a nightingale walks in, Roberta's eyes flash and the next thing Green remembers is been woken up by his rescuers.

The rogue Nightingale Alexandra believes that by gaining the cube's knowledge she can bring about a new golden age, but the cube is self-aware and could turn its knowledge against them or feed misinformation. Also the cube is compelled to obey the right signals even if the results are disastrous, like the incident on the Helides when the Nightingale sent a signal to turn the crew into those creatures. Alexandra believes that if one of them – Roberta - can be the host to the cube's memory store then the information can be controlled safely. Davidson, however, wants to leave, realising the potential danger Roberta represents to Nerva and the other stations. Davidson, using her new found knowledge and skills, builds a small ship for herself in the Mab's hanger, intending to travel to Earth's old colonies where no one from the stations can reach her. As she launches the ship, Alexandra and Roberta attack it using codes they've acquired form Green. Davidson's ship is damaged. Malcom and crew fire back but Roberta and Alexandra are protected by a shield. Davidson retaliates by hacking into their cybernetic implants, knocking them out. A few moments later, Davidson's ship splits into two, the two halves having been held together by a ribbon off energy, and they shoot off at high velocity.

Malcom, Munro and the others realise they've just witness the old FTL system that the empire used.

Alexandra and Roberta are arrested; Malcom goes back to his quarters on the Mab and finds a recorded message from Davidson. That reveals to him the location of an unknown facility on Mercury.

Broken Shell – sample chapters

Earth 3998AD

A small cargo ship is spotted heading towards Mars. Captain Malcolm, in command of the frigate Mab, is sent out to investigate by his superiors on Nerva. After an intense battle he soon finds himself wrapped in a plot that threatens to destroy his home and restore a long silent giant.

Chapter 1

Why me? Captain Malcolm thought as he approached the starboard airlock of the frigate Mab. Two crew members gave their captain a quick salute as he walked in. He waited for the chamber to unlock and walked across to the cargo ship Helides forty meters away.

The Helides was a civilian cargo ship, aligned to no authority, trading its goods freely between the stations around Earth. It had been sighted heading for Mars - an old colony that fell into anarchy centuries ago, a dangerous place full of the worst of humanity, according to those who lived on the other stations. The people of Mars were very interested in - and would pay good money for - any tech or substance to give them an edge over the stations. And for that reason, any ship going there from Earth was stopped and searched. The Helides had been detected as it passed through the space of the edge station of Nerva, and the Mab - being the nearest patrol ship – had been ordered to intercept the ship and search for any contraband, as was custom.

Once on board the Helides he was met by his counterpart, Captain Connors, a large man with a small round face, wearing a clean civilian dark blue uniform with gold accents along the arms and neck.

'Captain Connors,' greeted Malcom.

'Captain Malcom,' Connors replied with a calm voice, although his face was slightly uneased.

'Love the décor. Your ship,' Malcom went on in the same tone, Connors shooting him a sarcastic glance, 'was tracked heading for Mars several days ago, and despite repeated warnings to return to station space for inspection you have not changed your course. My Security teams are sweeping your ship for any illegal goods or dangerous substances. Your crew are also subject to searches. If they don't object and we find nothing out of the ordinary we can go our separate ways. Sound good?' asked Malcom, not bothering to keep the frustration out of his voice. As vital as they were, he hated patrol missions.

'Agreed but, ah, Captain. May I have a

word with you? On your ship, I mean?'

Connors sounded nervous, glancing at two of his crewmen who were busy being searched.

Malcolm raised an eyebrow.

'May I ask why?'

'I'd prefer it,' Connors replied hurriedly, 'if we talked away from my crew.'

Wanting to sell them out, Malcom thought.

He'd seen it before countless times and hated such men. He'd throw Connors out the airlock now if he could. But he'd see what the man had to say. He gestured towards the airlock and the two men walked side by side down the corridor, but before they reached it Connors started coughing and quivering violently.

'Damn it, I'm too late,' he groaned. 'Malcom! Get away from me and seal the airlock behind you. Quickly, man!'

Connors collapsed to the floor, began convulsing, and before Malcom eyes started glowing a sickly yellow. His convulsions stopped, and before Malcolm could step away Connors got lithely to his feet and quickly grappled Malcom by his uniform, pinning him to the wall of the airlock.

'Forgive me, I can't stop it!' he wailed.

Shots came from the frigate's side of the airlock as Malcolm's crewmen aimed at Connors, desperately trying not to hit their captain or breach the hull. One shot struck home and knocked Connors off balance, forcing him to release his grip on Malcolm,

Malcolm immediately rolling the several meters towards his crewmen, unholstering his energy pistol and aiming for Connors' head. He missed, but caught Connors square in the chest - a small hole appeared on Connors' uniform but he didn't fall, and continued to face Malcom down. Worse, Connors was sprouting a metallic tail, its barbed edges tearing his uniform to shreds.

'What the hell?' Malcom gasped, continuing to point his gun at Connors - or whatever the hell he was - Malcolm's crew members still beside him, exchanging nervous glances.

A voice came through his comm unit, direct into his ear.

'Sir, more security is on the way...'

Stall for time, he thought, *don't care how strong he is, he won't last long against a trained security team.*

Malcom glanced past Connors and could see flashes from energy weapons on the Helides side of the airlock window. It looked like Connors' crew were in trouble too, but Malcolm's men came first.

'Crewmen! Focus your shots...' Malcolm began but, before he could finish, Connors charged.

'Quickly! Back to the Mab!' Malcom shouted, his men carrying out a tactical retreat, covering each other with blasts from their energy weapons as they backed off, slowing Connors' advance until they reached the door, Malcom waiting until the last second to get behind the door just as Connors lunged.

'Seal the door!' Malcom barked, his men obeying, the doors closing but not quick enough, the top half of Connors' body cinched at the waist. He howled in pain, body glowing a bright yellow, face contorting into a strange animal shape, small metallic fangs pointing out of his mouth, and fingers transmogrifying into long claws that swiped futilely at Malcom and his crewmen but they were out of reach.

'Finish him!' Malcom shouted, and all three men blasted Connors' head until it was destroyed – but even headless, his arms were still swinging.

'Keep shooting!' Malcom bellowed over the gunfire, until what had been Captain Connors stopped moving, just as the backup security contingent arrived.

'Sir, we came as....what the hell is that?' asked the helmeted Security Sergeant Davidson, carrying her large pulse rifle and wearing full combat armour.

'Don't know, and right now don't care,' Malcolm responded. 'Get some of your men to take the corpse. Seal it away and post a guard on it. The rest of you - we have to get on board the Helides. We've men there who could be in trouble.'

His sergeant acknowledged the order and soon Malcom and the security team had unsealed the door to the Helides.

What met them was a bloodbath.

The large cargo bay into which they walked was slick with the blood of the four mangled corpses that lay at the centre of the room: three members of the security team, and one of the bizarre creatures. Behind some large barrels, Malcom's men found a barely alive Security Member from the Mab.

'Condition?' Malcom asked, as he crouched beside the man as a medic looked him over.

'Loss of blood and a gash on his chest,' the medic reported. 'His security vest must've stopped the blow from cutting too deep, but if he's to survive we need to take him back to the ship.'

'Do it.' said Malcom. He turned to the Sergeant.

'How many crew on the Helides?' he asked.

'Seven, sir.' she answered.

'Great. So two dead, five more to find. Get some more security here,' commanded Malcolm. 'We're going to have sweep the ship, deck by deck, room by room.

A short while later they found two of their men barricaded in a small room with three of the creatures dead at the door.

'Good work,' Malcolm said as he kicked the creatures out of the way and got the door open. 'Crewmen, what happened?'

'We don't know, Sir,' one answered. 'One minute we were searching the Helides crew and the next they were on the floor screaming and convulsing and turning into those...'

'Go on,' Malcolm demanded, the crewman swallowing.

'One of them took a swing at us but we managed to fire on them before they turned completely, and locked ourselves in, created a little bottleneck. But what's weird,' he went on, 'is that they didn't seem concerned with their own lives. They just wanted to kill us.'

He rubbed at his face and grimaced at the blood on his uniform.

'Did you see what happened to the other members off your team?' Malcolm asked.

'No, sir. It all happened so fast,' he said, with fatigue in his voice.

'Very well. Get back to the ship. Have the doctors have a look at you and clean yourselves up,' Malcom ordered.

'Aye, Sir!'

The two men nodded in relief and left for the Mab.

'Okay, let's keep going,' said Malcom, hearing through his comms that one of the other search teams had found another of the creatures' corpses next to an exposed energy conduit – it was badly burned, and appeared to have chucked itself deliberately at the core

One left, Malcom thought, as they approached the bowels of the ship.

The corridor was narrow, with pipes and cables clinging to the walls and roof, and the lighting was dimmer. The floor was nothing but metal grating with some pipes a few feet beneath it. The team could hear heavy footsteps in the distance; the Captain, Sergeant and her squad raised their weapons and moved carefully forward. The footsteps stopped, and the team continued cautiously.

Then, without warning, the floor beneath them collapsed, taking several members of the team with it. Down below, the last surviving creature was waiting for them: larger than the rest and with a more armoured appearance; its face far more feral, more wolflike, than the others; it's metallic fangs more prominent, and above its eyes were small slits that looked like they might be another set of eyes.

It took a swipe at one of the security team. He managed to block it with his rifle but no time to stop the tail piercing his stomach with a barb, the man going down with a cry of pain. A second later the creature took another swipe and took the man's head clean off its neck.

'Open fire!' Malcolm yelled, and from up above the rest of the team rained down a barrage of blue energy at the creature, until at last its armour started to give way, huge wounds opening up in its back, and before long it collapsed on top of another crewman too weak to roll out of the way.

'Down!' Malcolm commanded, his men dropping down and heaving the great bulk off their trapped crewman – he was gasping for breath, covered in blood, but none of it his.

'Alright?' Malcolm called from above.

'Aye, Sir!' he called back. 'Just a little

winded. Armour held off most of the weight.'

He shook his head, looked around the corridor, saw his beheaded comrade and another mess of body parts further down and no way to identify them. He'd been lucky, and sent a prayer up to his deity of choice.

Not so Malcolm, who didn't believe in luck, or deities.

'Damn it,' he whispered through clenched teeth. 'What the hell has been going on here?'

Chapter 2

A short while later, back in the Helides cargo ship, Captain Malcom, Sergeant Davidson and the other teams had regrouped. One of the Squad leaders approached Malcom with a small grey cube. It was suspended in a force field from his glove.

'Sir, we've searched the ship,' he said, 'and can't find anything unusual except this. We found it in Captain Connor's quarters. It's giving off a strange energy we can't identify.'

Malcom inspected it further: the cube appeared smooth and seamless apart from small engravings on the top and along the edges.

'Give it to Mr Munro. See what he can discover,' ordered Malcom. The Squad leader nodded and headed for the Mab.

Sergeant Davidson approached and removed her helmet. She had a mature face with sharp edges and lines; years of working security on ships had taken its toll, and she had a series of small scars from countless firefights. Her frail platinum hair was tied into a short pony tail.

'All the bodies are accounted for, Sir,' she reported. 'We're moving them to the Mab.'

'Excellent. So Sergeant, what happened to the Helides crew? Why attack us and why go to Mars?' pondered Malcom. With that he headed out the airlock to the Mab.

Walking the narrow corridors of the Mab,

Malcom went into his quarters, which weren't much bigger than those of the crew despite him being captain. His only real luxury was having his own bathroom. Space on the Mab was at a premium and every inch of the interior was used as efficiently as possible. The room was dimly lit with an orange glow. Malcom wandered to his desk chair and sat down to clear his head.

A few minutes later he opened the console, where he looked up the Helides and its history. Checking the Helides logs he discovered its last stop before heading to Mars was Station Hadrian, Nerva's neighbour with a major superiority complex. Malcom had had several dealings with ships from there and not all had turned out pleasantly. One of the crew logs reported that after they'd left Hadrian, Connors was starting to act strangely and trying to hide something from the rest of his crew, and looked wrecked with guilt.

Then he read Connors' own final written report:

We had a lucky escape from The Nightingale. She wants the cube. Why did I steal it? She's getting desperate - offering temptations and using my crew as hostages. I almost gave in at Hadrian. I can't risk bringing it to another station in case she finds me. Instead, I'll set course for Mars and hope my friends there can find a solution.

A later entry described the cube as humming, glowing an odd yellow and *talking* to the crew, telling them all their problem would go away if they embraced its harmony.

With that, Malcom got up and headed to Mr Munro's office. Munro was a civilian scientist from Nerva, drafted in to fill key roles otherwise missing from the ships roster. He was never happy about it, and made sure Malcom knew it. As Malcom stepped in to the room, his ears were hit with a cacophony of music that would drive angels mad. He, however, kept his composure. Munro was sitting at his table, which was cluttered with scientific instruments. In the middle was the strange cube.

Karlsen a junior officer, was with Munro as an unofficial assistant.

'Ah Captain! I was wondering when you'd get here!' Munro shouted over the music. He was a tall middle-aged man, wearing a light blue uniform and had bright crimson hair cut in a Mohawk. He had a small grin on his face

'Mr Munro, Mr Karlsen,' Malcom kept his voice raised but not angry, although internally he was picturing a million ways he could remove Munro's kidneys and sell them on. He approached the two men; Karlsen was looking a little sheepish and tried to do his best to look out of the way. Munro turned the music off.

'Oh please keep it on, I was rather enjoying it,' Malcolm said, with a slight sneer. 'So what is our mysterious cube?'

'As far as I can tell, just a cube,' Malcom gave Munro a glance and took a seat opposite him. 'Seriously, aside from the unusual energy signature which appears to be inert, I can't find anything wrong with it. The etching, however is very interesting.'

'Do tell,' said Malcom.

'They're written in a language used by the The Orthographik Order,' Munro paused to emphasise the inevitable follow up.

'Who are they? I've not heard of them,' said Karlsen. A stocky man with a youthful face, he'd shown an interest in science and history and been scooped up by Munro the second he found that out.

'I'm glad someone can still ask questions. Seriously, captain, your crew barely has the imagination of a gnat,' joked Munro

'Continue,' Malcom said quickly, wondering what would happen if he set Munro's hair on fire.

'Well, The Orthographik Order were obsessed with finding old technologies and using them for their own purposes,' Munro explained.

'Like The Nightingales?' asked Karlsen.

'Possibly. They were quite secretive; it's why they came up with their own language,' answered Munro.

'Interesting. Connors' log mentioned a Nightingale going after the cube,' said Malcom. 'Is it Old Empire tech?'

'Could be,' replied Munro. 'We know so little of the Old Empire. But the other thing about the Order is that they're from Vulcan,' he stated. Both Malcom and Karlsen looked at him with shock. Vulcan was one of the stations orbiting Earth, but went silent two centuries ago. Nothing coming from it since, and any ship going in never heard from again.

'So what does it say?' Malcom asked.

'Couldn't tell you,' said Munro. 'There are only a few who can read their language. One of the old records in Nerva's university might hold a clue,' Munro continued.

'It's our best lead,' said Malcom, and with that he ordered the ship to head back to Nerva.

Soon enough the Mab roared back towards Earth. Two days later the ship was passing close to the Moon, the frigate a shining blue light against the grey backdrop of the Moon's surface, making its way through the fields of scattered debris - remnants of an age of battles long forgotten. The Mab was elegant and smooth, wings folded back at an angle half way down the cabin body, two small engines at their tips, with two larger engines in the middle so it looked like a glider that has been moulded by strong winds. At the end of her body was her main engine. Unobtrusive gun turrets were mounted on the struts that served as bracers, and the overall appearance was of a clean and very efficient missile, as fast as it was nimble. The few windows on the ship were along the middle of her body looking out onto the wings and engines. The ship's airlock fitted perfectly with the shape of her forward section.

Malcom was on the Bridge; the Bridge of the Mab was located in the heart of the ship - a small room full of consoles and screens. Standing by the planning table at the back of the room, he was soon joined by his First officer, and Munro and Davidson.

'The doctor's report came in,' explained Malcolm. 'She said that the machine parts in bodies of the Helides crew were altered on a molecular level, causing their transformation.'

He found this worrying. These days every human had some form of cybernetic implant to help cope with life on the stations.

'Did the cube cause it?' wondered First Officer Green. A short man with trim cut hair; a man, Malcom thought, never happy unless he had something to complain about.

'Are we at risk?' Davidson asked

'It might not even be the cube,' Munro spoke up. 'Besides, it's harmless at the moment. I have it sealed in containment. Nobody can get near it.'

'Sir,' a Bridge crewman interrupted, 'I'm seeing strange activity from a debris field near the Moon's equator.'

'It's probably just an old mine drifting about,' snapped Munro. Malcom stared daggers at him

'Not unless an old mine can send a signal towards us, is three times our size and heading right for us,' the Bridge Officer retorted.

Emerging from the debris was a large wedge-shaped ship with two sets of wings at its top that were angled at forty-five degrees. It was black, with hints of violet laced over its hull, and between its wings was a large cannon that was half the ship's length, and that ship was charging up, aiming its canon straight at the Mab's centre. Malcom had never seen anything like it, though the colours matched Station Juno it didn't match anything they had.

'Battlestations!' Malcom ordered, and moved to the centre of the bridge and stood by the command consoles, attached himself to the railings using the clip on them. The enemy ship fired a dark purple energy beam - it lasted a short moment and then hit the Mab in her middle section, lacerating across her hull deep enough to create a breach. The impact rocked the crew and those who weren't secured went flying, crashing into the walls and roof, causing a great deal of injury.

'Sir, we've lost communication and our defence turrets are gone!' the Bridge Officer stated.

'Bring us around; get us out of that gun's firing arc.' Malcom ordered with a steady voice, maintaining his cool. He was in his element. The ship had stopped rocking and he glanced about the bridge. Some of the crew were down, including Green.

Davidson and Munro were clipped to the table and weren't badly shaken.

A small pod launched from the enemy ship and landed in the hull breach.

The intruder alert alarm went off in the bridge.

'Davidson, get down there,' Malcolm

commanded.

Davidson nodded and moved out.

'Weapons stations! Return fire, target that main gun and their power systems,' Malcom directed.

The Mab had now manoeuvred beside the enemy's port side and opened fire with her remaining guns. The enemies' defensive turrets blocked much of the incoming fire but some shots hit home and blew holes in the side of the enemy.

'Helmsman, bring us around for another pass,' Malcolm commanded.

'Aye Sir,' he acknowledged.

Davidson made her way from the rear of the ship, making a quick stop at the armoury and getting her equipment, meeting up with her team.

'Our sensors show the intruder is going to Munro's lab,' reported one of her team.

'Of course it is,' she said dryly. 'Let's go.'

She walked steadily toward the lab, the corridor's lighting dimming; the impact from the attack having damaged some of the Mab's power systems.

Once they reached the lab they took defensive positions around the entrance. Further down the corridor, a robed figure with the same colours as the strange ship appeared. Davidson took a closer look: the figure had an androgynous appearance, its skin dark grey, with glowing purple eyes, glowing strands of the same purple going down its face, highlighting its cheeks, neck and body. Although it was completely mechanical its mouth looked almost human.

It continued on it slow methodical walk to the lab.

An Avatar. Oh shit. Davidson thought.

She opened her coms by pressing an embedded implant in her neck.

'Captain, we have an Avatar.'

'Proceed with caution,' Malcom responded. His voice sounded wrong.

'Don't have to tell me twice,' Davidson murmured to herself. The figure was now just ten meters away; it continued walking and then gave a slight nod of its head – and a sudden unseen force knocked Davidson and her team several feet back on the floor. She picked her gun back up and shot the Avatar in the shoulder.

It had no effect, its shoulder just absorbed the energy from the shot.

She fired again, but still it wasn't affected.

The ship rocked again, the Mab had taken another hit.

The lights in the corridor were almost out.

'Please don't, we would hate to hurt you more. We just want the artefact.'

The Avatar spoke calmly, with a horrible gravelly voice but then changed to a precisic imitation of Malcom's voice. Davidson tapped her neck again, realising it hadn't been her captain she'd spoken to a moment ago. The

Avatar inclined its head.

Davidson charged her weapons to maximum, her team followed suit and they all fired at once. The impact would have torn anything else to shreds, but again the Avatar just stood there unfazed.

'As you wish,' it said calmly and looked at Davidson more intently – and then she and her team were pinned to the floor, unable to move, struggling to breathe.

The Avatar walked into the lab.

Back on the now smoking bridge, Malcom continued the battle. He had a slight gash on his forehead. Having taken more damage to her hull, there were now several burning breaches across the Mab's body, she manged to outmanoeuvre the enemy and was behind them with a clean shot of primary engines.

'All power to forward weapons,' Malcom ordered. The crewmen acknowledged the order. 'Fire!'

The Mab unleashed a torrent of blue energy at the enemy ship; the enemy had few defensive weapons at its rear and almost all of the Mab's fury got through. The ship's engines was completely destroyed but the Mab's attack didn't end there, several more volleys creating large hull breaches that caused secondary explosions throughout the ship.

Davidson felt the force leave her and started to move and breathe again; she grabbed her gun and ran into the laboratory. It was a mess, everything was on the floor. The Avatar was kneeling over as if something had just knocked the wind out of it. Davidson couldn't know it, but the invulnerability cloak granted it by the enemy ship had been taken out by the latest attack and, when Davidson raised her weapon and fired and hit it in the back, this time the Avatar flinched. It turned to face her. If it were human it would've looked shocked and surprised, almost afraid. It dived behind the nearest table, extended its arm and fired a concentrated beam from its hand towards Davidson.

She ducked out of the way and returned the favour. Her weapon blew a hole through the table and struck the Avatar in the side of its chest. It fired again at Davidson in desperation; then rolled out its cover and smashed the cube from its containment casing. It took the cube which started glowing a bright yellow and making a loud, high pitched noise that suddenly turned into music, like angels singing a hymn. Davidson had never heard anything so beautiful and was taken away by it.

She shrugged herself out of the trance-like state and saw that the Avatar was equally distracted so she aimed her gun and fired at its head.

It went down with a hard bang.

The cube landed on the floor, the singing getting louder and the glow more intense.

Davidson shielded her eyes with her arm as the glowing light from the cube directed itself toward her and started to envelop her. She felt her body changing, as if were being renewed; all the years of fighting and injuries were washed away and she felt young again. Suddenly a figure walked through the light and grabbed her by the neck and lifted her up.

It was the Avatar, its head was still partially intact.

'It not for you!!' it shouted, still with Malcom's voice but more distorted.

With her renewed strength, Davidson reached into the holes her weapon had created and started tearing out anything she thought felt important. The Avatar squeezed around her neck, but its grip was failing; with its other hand it took a swing at Davidson's head. She manged to move her shoulder to take the hit instead.

The light grew stronger: now it enveloped them both.

There was a bright flash.

The music was gone, and so was the Avatar, leaving Davidson unconscious on the floor.

'Sir, I'm reading a strange energy build up in the enemy ship,' said the Bridge Officer, with fatigue in his voice. Malcom considered this, then sudden realisation hit him: the enemy ship was going to self-destruct rather than allow its self to be boarded.

'Get us away fast!' he shouted.

The Mab started to back off, and the enemy vessel exploded in a shower of scattering debris. Some of hit the Mab, putting more holes into her damaged body.

The explosion caught up and she strained under the pressure; the hull creaked and groaned, until eventually the explosion passed and she flew on.

Malcom breathed a sigh relief, looked to his crew.

He felt nothing but pride for them.

'Good work everybody.' He said with a smile. 'Now let's go home.'

A while later, he visited the Med Bay and saw to his injured crew.

He'd lost twenty-seven in the battle, and many more were injured.

He approached the now young Davidson, who was still unconscious lying on a bed.

'What happened to her?' Malcom asked concerned.

'I can't say. Her body is shielded from all my instrument,' the doctor replied.

Munro walked in beside him.

'The cube's gone,' he said solemnly. 'There's no trace of it.'

Karlsen was one of those killed.

'He was a good lad.'

They stood in silence for a few moments.

A few hours later, Malcom was sitting in his quarters contemplating the previous few days. There was still the unexplained transformations of the Helides crew. He was convinced the cube lay at the root of it, but the cube was gone, and the last person who might have seen it was unconscious in the Med Bay.

'Captain Malcom, we're approaching Nerva. We should be docking shortly,' a voice called through the coms

'Thank you, Helmsman,' Malcom responded.

The Mab flew towards her destination. She was still heavily damaged, but Malcom would be dammed if they towed her in.

Earth was a shining blue ball, the dawn just starting creep over the planet.

Against the sun, Station Nerva was growing larger by the second. It was a miss mash of old and new; the once smooth, elegant design of the old defence station now covered in small habitats and bulky inelegant skyscrapers like barnacles on a ship's hull. There was a Mag Rail system, and then there was the three-kilometre-long spike of its gun barrel - that also served as a docking station – that had the appearance of a long metallic bill, straight as a rod, but cleft down the centre as if sliced through by the sharpest, thinnest most accurate of knives.

It was bespoke engineering at its greatest; a masterpiece of precision using methods of construction long forgotten.

'Home at last,' Malcolm said to himself.

A Family Outing

By Pam Rowe

Husband and wife, Longfo and Winglee, were on a family outing with their children Changfo and Pingfo. It was Chinese New Year and the family always felt homesick for their native Thailand at this time. They had come across to Europe as part of the wave of Boat People; a young unmarried couple, they'd been in a camp of ex-RAF houses in Watton Norfolk before being rehoused with the help of the charity *Save the Children.*

Their own children had arrived later in their lives, and it was the first time the family had returned to Thailand for a holiday since that stage in their lives ten to fifteen years before. The children looked in awe at the colourful clothes worn by the Thai people, who always wore a lot of red as it was considered lucky at this time of the year. It was the year of the Monkey, and festivities were well started with a Dragon dancing around the streets, writhing and twisting as it made its way through the crowd. It was followed by a procession of people in a parade, either dancing with the Dragon or sitting or standing on floats and waving to the crowd as it wound its way to the end of the route.

The whole scene enthralled the children because the culture of their forefathers was very new to them, as they were very European and it was their first experience of their homeland.

The procession ended with cages of animals taking up the rear, including tigers and lions, horses dancing behind them dressed in colourful coats and with plaited manes and straw hats. Following these came penguins hopping and wobbling along, looking very dapper in their natural plumage of black and white as if they were in evening dress.

Along the way, cafés and restaurants were offering lots of food, mainly Thai curries and other delicacies, all adding to the atmosphere of the day.

Hours later, on return of the family to the hotel and the children were getting into bed, the whole day was talked about and all agreed it was a really memorable day.

Script Style Exercise

3 Min Dialogue

By Debbie Ruppenthal

Jimmy enters the office where Monica is sat at the desk staring at a computer screen

He props himself against the door frame

JIMMY   We're in big trouble.

When she doesn't answer immediately he walks towards her and perches on the desk where Monica is working

MONICA Uh huh

Jimmy sets his jaw in irritation

JIMMY   Were you listening to me, Monica? We're in big trouble.

He emphasises the word big

JIMMY   Deep shit.

Monica turns her head, still not really listening

MONICA What were you saying? Something about being double?

Jimmy stands up, unable to control his frustration

JIMMY   For fuck's sake, Monica! You never listen!

Jimmy is almost shouting now, shaking his head, exasperated

JIMMY   I said trouble, for god's sake!

In deep shit. Fucked.

Monica takes her gaze from the PC screen and she focuses on Jimmy, taking in the red face, the spit in the corner of his mouth

MONICA Slow down, Jim. Go back a bit. What's happened?

Jimmy takes a breath and pulls the office chair out from the desk beside her and sits on it heavily

He takes a deep breath

JIMMY Hassan has been on the phone. He thinks they may be onto us. He had a call. Someone asking questions.

He rests his elbows on the desk and leans his head into his hands

MONICA Who's been asking questions? What questions? You know what a panicker Hassan is. It's probably nothing. Probably some cousin wanting a job, trying to muscle his way in

She tosses her loose hair, puts a stray bit behind her ear

Jimmy lifts his head from his hands and looks at her

There's a pause before he speaks again

He's calmer now

JIMMY No. It wasn't a bloody cousin. It was a fraud officer. From the tax office. He was asking some *routine questions*, except they weren't very routine.

Jimmy smiles

He shrugs

His shoulders drop

His voice is emotionless now

JIMMY   He wants to make an appointment

Monica stands up

She walks behind Jimmy and rest her hands on his chair back

She touches his shoulder with her left hand and squeezes

MONICA Look Jim. We're good. Watertight. Hassan might be wetting his knickers a bit, but there's nothing they're gonna find out.

Monica turns the chair so that Jim is facing her

MONICA Let whoever it is make an appointment with me. As financial director Hassan should be there, but as CEO I should answer any questions. Honestly, don't worry. We can deal with this. I don't need you going all Rita Heyworth on me now

Jimmy looks at Monica directly

Her self-assuredness has always impressed him

Always made him feel like he should trust her

He gives a small nod

JIMMY   Ach, maybe you're right, Mon. Maybe I over-reacted a bit, but Hassan was badly shaken. I don't think he'd handle too much questioning, even if it was nothing to worry about.

He stands up and grabs Monica around the waist, pulling her into him

Monica pulls back slightly and tilts her head to look up at Jimmy

MONICA Now that's more like it, lover boy

She's smiling, making light of the situation

MONICA I've never thought of you as weakling.

She presses her body into him and kisses him on the cheek, then pulls away and walks towards the filing cabinet to the right of the door

Jimmy watches the swing of her hips, and the swish of her skirt and feels aroused

He follows behind her and presses his groin into the small of her back

JIMMY   Nothing pathetic about this.

He pushes into her suggestively

Monica opens the top draw of the filing cabinet and shunts Jimmy backwards

She flicks through the suspension files and pulls an orange foolscap folder from one of them and rest it against her chest

MONICA Now, now, hot stuff. What did we agree about us and the office?

She closes the draw, moving into it as it closes, leaving a gap between herself and Jimmy

She turns around and leans back on the filing cabinet provocatively, lifting one leg to prop against it, which lifts her skirt

MONICA That particular bad boy can wait until tonight.

She winks and transfers the file to her right hand which she drops to her side

She goes to walk out of the office and then

changes her mind

She throws the file towards Jimmy like a Frisbee

Jimmy catches the file

MONICA Here. See what you make of that. It might put your mind at ease.

She looks pleased with herself, puts her hands on her hips

MONICA When you've read it, shred it.

She puts a finger to her mouth and concentrates.

MONICA What day is it? Thursday? That's fine. Mrs Mop's will be in tonight, they'll empty the shredder.

MONICA We'll both have a chat with Hassan tomorrow. Can you get that in the diaries, sweetie?

Monica is distracted again

She turns away before Jimmy answers and walks out through the open door

EXIT Monica

Jimmy looks at the file he's holding

He looks up at Monica walking away

He frowns

Being a personal assistant is all very well, but Monica can be a bit of a diva

He mumbles a response which there's no way she'll hear

JIMMY Sure. No sooner said than done. As always.

A Lone Survivor

Based on the Painting *Ritorno dal Bozco, 1890,* by Giovanni Segantini

By Bryan Rowe

Friedrich had been following the snow bound trek across the barren wasteland. The village ahead blended into the bleak landscape. He was weary of pulling the sledge loaded with a huge log from a dead oak tree covered in gnarled branches clinging to the wood like the torn limbs from a reclining torso. Death to him was ever near.

It was late afternoon, dusk would soon be falling and the silence surrounding the small village ahead was deafening. No sign of smoke from the cottage chimneys, no distant voices or the sight of children playing. The grey church steeple stood tall like a finger pointing to heaven. The sounds of happy chatter and laughter following weddings and christenings echoed from the past in his memory. This was a thriving village, now complete desolation. He noticed even the birds that continually flew criss-crossing the skyline were silent. Maybe this was due to the ever invading darkness that was closing in.

Friedrich had set out that morning to collect wood from the forest some six kilometres away, now tired and exhausted, his feet were swollen and sore from walking on the hard ground with the cold gripping him like an iron fist. He dreaded the loneliness of the night ahead.

How could such a fate befall him? He could hardly call himself lucky when on that terrible day two weeks ago Serbian soldiers had descended on the village, rounded up all the men and boys to take them off to a mass execution site. The womenfolk terrified by the cull and the threat of rape had fled for their lives taking their children and elders with them. Was it providence that he was away collecting wood that day? He would never forget that scene in front of him when returning to the village. From a distance he had watched the complete termination of his homestead.

For several days Friedrich had hidden in a large cave in the hillside near the village. Too frightened to move , the endless, deadly silence all around eventually persuaded him to return to his cottage but his constant fear was would the soldiers return, what had happened to his wife and family, were they safe in one of the nearby towns? The gravity of his present existence amidst the familiar surroundings of the village made him realise the full impact of being in no-man's land.

Gone, But Not Forgotten

By Laura Kirk

It was cold. The air was dry and dusty. I saw no light, only darkness. My hands, written immobile. The tangy taste of metal flooded my mouth and my first instinct was to swallow.

Lifting my tired and heavy cranium caused my neck to crack. Relief washed over my body. I could tell that I was on my knees, a wooden pole keeping my bound hands in place so that my escape was impossible.

I heard the whinnies of horses and the laughter of men, I knew that these sounds did not belong to my Tribe. *Where am I?* I asked myself. Images flashed through my mind. Dark grey smoke that dared to engulf me and fill my lungs. Fire that never seemed to cease in its path of destruction. Red rivers that never stopped spilling over my feet.

The rain of my eyes began to fall upon my mocha skin. Was I hurt? Yes, but my pain did not deserve tears. Was I scared? No, I never found myself to be a man of fear.

I dropped my head and sighed heavily, my voice came out in shakes. The sensation of my long black hair brushing my shoulders and cheeks made the touched skin itch.

A stream of light flooded my line of vision, causing my optics to shut while my brows furrowed in pain. Words that I did not understand were spoken and I was lifted from my position, my hands free from the pole but the rope still dug into my skin.

Dragged, shoved and pulled into the sunlight, the breeze that caressed my body held the scent of smoke and blood. Panic lined my features as I could only see white. The colour soon faded to green, red and black.

Fire. The orange flames danced upon the wood of our forests. M tears had a reason to fall. I witnessed my once peaceful and tranguil Tribe being slaughtered before being thrown on to the flames that engulfed their lifeless bodies. The smell of burning flesh filled my nose and my face twisted in disgust. Deafening sounds occurred and made me flinch. The white men dragged me to a specific spot, laughing.

These men took away everything I had. My family, my home and soon my life.

I was filled with fear and peace, all at the same time.

It all seemed surreal and yet devastatingly real.

My death was inevitable.

Why must we fear death if we all know that we cannot change it?

My gaze followed the charred trees to the sky where no chaos interrupted the clouds.

A bald eagle soared above me, screeching and making eye contact with my brown gaze. A beautiful creature in a messed up world. I prayed there and then that the creature would soar and rule the skies forever, watching the land change and develop. I prayed that it would keep the land safe from these white men that came without warning only to erase us.

As if it heard my prayer, it gave a screech. My lips formed a smile as I spoke my final words

'Thank you.'

There was no sound, no pain and no regret. I simply returned to the darkness where familiar faces formed and embraced me.

Over time, more of my people joined us and we found ourselves soaring above the trees.

Watching.

Keeping our land wild and free, like it should be.

Peadra

By Josephine S. J. Sumner

Peadra lit the candle in the hearth. She did so with a studious grace. Her thick, red hair picked up the light from the candle and glimmered with flaming tones. Her eyes shone amber.

It was the end of the summer. Outside the butterflies had flitted over the golden rod, thistles, wild thyme and birds foot trefoil and the sun shone. The sea was a deep, brilliant blue and the hills rose mistily over the firth.

Now, after that day of sun she was sun kissed and happy, for that gem of a day had refreshed and revived her spirits. Heron had glided to and fro and stood for ages on the rocks. The shags had a colony not far away. In the distance she could see the lighthouse with its red and white swirls. Maybe she would walk there one day. She sat in the small, Spartan croft and thought of this solitude which she had sought – solitude – alone.

Why would anyone wish to be alone? Because then there were no pressures of another person's wants, intrigues, no one demanding of your time. Sometimes you sought company but sometimes it smothered you or personalities smothered you and the more it happened the harder it was to stand firm in what you believed.

Peadra had always thought she had strength. She had withstood many things and carried on, a little scarred, much scarred perhaps because, latterly, she hadn't been able to distinguish whether it was conditioning making her respond in a certain way.

Who was she? Somebody called her dynamic recently and someone else called her pathetic. Again, she was called a ravishing red head and then a red head that looked well ravished. There is a world of difference between those two remarks. She could be both dynamic and attractive or pathetic and past it – it's all in the perception. We all have the mouse and lion in us, which one is fostered? She thought most men prefer women to be mice to their lion. The lioness is stronger and fiercer than the lion!

She seemed to have lost herself in bringing up children, the core, the unique thing that everyone had. It had not been easy to obtain this space; she'd fought for it. Recently though, she'd never stopped screaming at the kids. One day she'd screamed so much her head had started bubbling and she saw stars. It was as if she was turning into a monster, quite the opposite of a warm, nurturing mother. The day-to-day grind and monotony drained her. Mothers sacrificed so much of themselves and never received any thanks, it was all taken for granted and your brain could go numb. She felt like a piece of furniture, somewhat scuffed and battered and not at all appreciated.

This gracious solitude, this beautiful day, which she's absorbed and expanded in like a flower opening up to the sun, was not to be broken by another's frustrations, another's problems, another's demands. Its undiluted brilliance would flow on into her dreams. There had been no jarring – no scarring. She stared into the candle and wished for this clarity and buoyancy to remain – wished very strongly to keep it there in the inter-weavings of society and family that would have to be faced again.

It had been so hot and at one point she'd plunged into the sea and it was beautifully cool and refreshing. The throngs of seaweed, the lap of the sea, the heat of the sun, the butterflies, the flowers and birds, the quiet, the wonderful liquid quiet. To have time to think and sift and sort.

The murmur of the sea, the distant murmur, murmur, murmur, murmur...

Swimming in the sea again. Swimming right out into the North Sea and the current pulling, pulling hard, pulling, and pulling. She resisted in a panic, inwardly screaming *No!* Trying vainly to regain the shore until her arms were tired, aching so much, yet another final attempt, but she was tired, deep down tired.

Feebly jerking legs and arms in the direction of the far receding shore and then giving up and drifting slowly downwards, down into the cool, cool depths of the sea.

The sea flowed over her, the sea flowed

in her, the sea encompassed her and called her its own. There was a tinkling of tiny bells, tinkling a kind of silvery tune that quivered and wavered, spun and spiralled and Peadra felt that it entered her soul and filled it with a vitality that would last for several lifetimes.

She opened her eyes.

A Father Apart

By Bryan Rowe

Omah took a deep breath and looked over to the mountains in the distance, sighed, and looked down at the sprawling mass of people and constant movement in the packed streets of the city below. He was looking out of the window of his son's flat on the top floor of the building. This was one of his rare visits to the city and still something of a culture shock. As a farmer-shepherd all his life, he and his wife had lived within the mountains and plains of the remote countryside of Eastern Peru where the yellow rocks of the surrounding hills were bleached yellow by the sun.

Static, unlike the streets below.

Always static.

The temperature could change dramatically day to night, unlike the city, where he found the constant heat and pollution unbearable

His son Joseph entered the room and handed him a mug of coffee. Joseph was dressed in clothes that matched the modern day businessman's identity: blue pin-striped shirt, dark grey alpaca trousers with the obligatory knife edge crease. In contrast, Omah had never been accustomed to wearing any other clothing than hand-made shirts woven from goats' hair, and loose cotton trousers that gave him the personal freedom for walking the hills in the blazing heat.

Omah could not understand why his son wore the black, very thick-framed spectacles that made him look so officious and distant.

'How long have you been wearing glasses?' Omah enquired. 'None of the rest of the family have had any problems with their sight.'

Joseph's expression showed that he was annoyed with his father's question.

'They add an air of authority to my business negotiations,' he replied. 'You've no idea how many meetings and high profile interviews I have to do these days.'

Omah took a sip of coffee and looked his son in the face.

'You shouldn't have to rely on such things to further your existence on this earth. You are a man in your own right.'

Joseph took his glasses off and rubbed them with his handkerchief.

'You don't know what you're talking about.' he grumbled, unable to meet his father's eye.

'You were so skilled with the sheep as a boy,' Omah went on, 'and how good you were at watching the skies for signs of changes in the weather.' He glanced towards the window at the smog haze beyond. 'You were always much more help to me than your bothers. It's a great regret for me that you felt you couldn't carry on the family tradition by staying and working alongside me in the homestead.'

'Oh for heavens sake!' Joseph interrupted. 'Please don't start going on about the old traditions!'

Omah felt the heat rise in his throat.

'At least you wouldn't need glasses if you'd stayed at home! My sight as an old man is as good as ever, all thanks to having to follow the distant paths made by the sheep and keeping a lookout for the wild packs of jackals that roam the hills.'

His words were angry, bitter as the coffee he finished in one gulp, turning back to the window. This time he saw his own reflection in the glass; the skin of his face was white and lined like parchment. He then looked again over to the distant mountains he had loved all his life and regretted it was apparently so lost to his son, but hoped too his son was not lost to him because of it.

Circles

by Rebecca Nankivell

Based on the painting 'Love Letters 1984-1988' by Howard Hodgkin

Postcard 1
1ˢᵗ January 1984

Hi Magda,

I was given you as the one to write to. My name is Ronnie and I'm based in the outer circle at present. Hope you will write to me.

Yours truly,
Ronnie

Postcard 2
4ᵗʰ February 1984

Dear Ronnie,

Yes, I am happy to reply to your card. How did you know my name? I've been in the inner circle since last month. Don't know if I'm allowed to write this, but you have to get out of the outer circle. To do this, spin to the edge every opportunity you get and jump. Have no fear as one of your jumps will land you in the inner.

Love Magda

Postcard 3
12th March 1984

Hi Magda,
Thanks for replying and the advice.
I jumped.
Still here though.
Yours truly,
Ronnie

Postcard 4
15th March 1984

Dear Ronnie,
You've got to keep jumping!
Do it now!
Love Magda

Postcard 5
4th June 1984

Hi Magda,
I hope you are well.
I didn't want to write again until I was in the inner circle.
I felt I'd be letting you down.

Still stuck here in the outer circle.

But God help me, as I've jumped 77 times.

Yours truly,
Ronnie

Editor's note: Postcards 6 to 13 are missing from The Love Letter Collection, but we can deduce from previous and later correspondence that Ronnie and Magda fell in love and spent the next year trying to reach other.

Postcard 14
15th May 1985

Dear Ronnie,
Where are you?
Love Magda

Postcard 15
2nd June 1985

Ronnie,
Where are you?
I haven't heard from you in a while.
Are you still in the blue?
I've made it to a splash of ochre.
Don't ask me how I got here.
I dunno.
But here I am out of the inner circle and to be honest I'm shitting myself.

Wish you were here.
Love Magda

Postcard 16
5th December 1985

Hi Magda,
Finally got your cards.
Dunno what's wrong with the post.
Keep smiling if you can.
I'm trying to find you.
I'm in the deep blue.
It's definitely getting darker.
Yours truly,
Ronnie

Postcard 17
10th January 1986

Magda!
I made it!
I'm in the deepest blue pushing out to ochre.
But there's no one here.
Love Ronnie

Postcard 18
23rd February 1986

Dearest Ronnie,

Thank god you made it!

You've seven months to get to the next circle.

They say the salmon are bad so avoid them.

Stick to the edges.

I'm waiting.

Love Magda

Postcard 19
13th May 1986

Hi Magda,

Thanks for the advice.

Got here a bit too late.

In a bad way.

Ronnie

Postcard 20
19th June 1986

Dear Ronnie,

How badly are you hurt?

Where are you?

Is anyone with you?

Love Magda

Postcard 21
31st August 1986

Hi Magda,
Have got to ochre stage one.
Very steep here.
Keep slipping.
Got dangerously close to returning to the
blue.
Send me courage.
Love Ronnie

Postcard 22
14th September 1986

Dearest Ronnie,
Haven't been able to write.
Concessions are taking place.
But never give up.
Love Magda

Postcard 23
April 1st 1987

Hi Magda,
Don't know if you'll get this.
I'm in the tunnel.
It's very dark.
Yours for ever,
Ronnie

Postcard 24

5th June 1987

Dear Ronnie,
I can't help any longer.
It's got real bad.
Sorry.
All my love Magda

Postcard 25
8th July 1987

Hi Magda,
Finally out of the tunnel.
Where are you?
Yours truly,
Ronnie

Postcard 26
14th Ocotber 1987

My darling Ronnie,
Look out for me and catch me if you can.
It will mean everything if you can.
Last chance saloon.
Love Magda

Postcard 27
16th Novemebr 1987

Darling Magda,

I look for you all the time.
Where are you?
Love Ronnie

Postcard 28
19th December 1987

Ronnie!
Catch me quick.
I'm falling!

Postcard 29
29th December 1987

Magda,
I'm on the cusp.
Jump and I'll catch you.

Postcard 30
2nd January 1988

Magda,
Where are you?
You've got to jump!
R
xxx

Postcard 31

[Undated]

I fell, Ronnie.
Don't try to follow.
Be safe.
Love Magda

Postcard 32
27th January 1988

Where are you my love?
Tell me and I'll find you.
I'll find you.
Ronnie

Editor's note: this is the last postcard we could find. We don't know where either Magda or Ronnie ended up. We can only hope they made it out to the pink.

Reliving The Day

By Pam Rowe

'Watch out, Mary!'

Elizabeth gasped as she watched her young daughter heading at speed towards the disaster that lay ahead of her as she skated around a full ice rink on this half term holiday. It was even more unnerving for her as she was very aware of the emptiness that returned each year to haunt her. It had been made even harder today as she had heard the hymn *All things Bright and Beautiful* played on the organ within the church as she passed outside. Although it was a lovely children's hymn, it had very sad memories because it had been sung at the funeral of her first born on this very day twelve years ago.

Every year she made the pilgrimage past the church so that she could be alone to relieve the emotions of her grief as she had never forgotten the enormity of the event. Losing someone you love is always hard, but when it is your own baby daughter it causes pain that is impossible to bear.

After her second child was born, Elizabeth had tried to protect her, always worrying about any activity that Mary had wanted to do. She'd finally relented when her daughter pleaded with her to learn to skate, as she wanted to be like her school girl friend who was training to be a professional skater and had already entered the European Championships and qualified for the World Championships in Switzerland in November this year.

Moments later, the inevitable happened as she watched the commotion on the rink where several children had fallen in a bunch and Mary, skating too fast, went head over heels over them, hitting her head and losing consciousness.

Elizabeth rushed to her side and cuddled her child while an ambulance was sent for. Mary was carried into the ambulance on a stretcher and they made good speed to the nearest hospital. On the journey, Elizabeth was beside herself. Here she was trying to stay calm in this present situation while reliving the experiences of twelve years ago when she was travelling to the same hospital with her baby daughter who at that time was being resuscitated by the ambulance men. She had found Joan in her cot, not breathing but still warm, when she had gone to feed her. There had been no indication that this four month old baby was ill for she'd thrived well from birth. The ambulance men had managed to get her to breathe again, but she died later in hospital.

The ordeal of the funeral with the tiny little coffin and the children's hymn still stayed with her and filled her with horror.

The events of this present day were so

upsetting that it was making her feel quite ill and faint, and she was afraid she was going to pass out; all she could see within the dizziness was a large hole in the ice where Mary's tumble had occurred, into which she would willingly have jumped if it would have saved her daughter from this awful fall.

They arrived at the hospital in due course and treatment was commenced at once and, after a few hours, Mary regained consciousness and greeted her mother quite lucidly and was surprised at the events that had happened.

By this time Mary's father had arrived at the hospital as well and both parents were at the bedside when the doctor walked in.

'Mary has done well to regain consciousness so quickly after her injuries, but I would like her to stay overnight to monitor her condition. I'll re-assess her in the morning to see if she can go home.'

After the little girl had had something to eat and was settled in her bed in the brightly decorated children's ward and was resting, Elizabeth shut her eyes and said a little prayer to thank God for saving her child.

The Thin Edge of the Slice

By Josephine S. J. Sumner

February 6th

I'm sitting in my room again. I don't want to watch telly, I watch it all the time when I'm not at school in the winter. In the summer I ride my bike. I go to Balintore and Portmahomack and swim if it's sunny, with my pal Susan. I love the summer. Sometimes I cycle to Loch Eye – it's not so far. In the autumn the greylag geese come, thousands of them and they are always flying over Tain where I live. I'm eleven and nearly two months old. It was my birthday just before Christmas, well the 19th of December.

I wish it would snow. That's what I like about the winter, the snow, but I think it's too near the sea here to have very much – someone said.

Mum is out and Ron is downstairs. Mum and me live with Ron. Ron isn't my dad. My dad ran off with another woman mum said and she doesn't want to speak about him. Some kids see their dad, Susan does sometimes but I don't. I think that he'd take me swimming and give me presents and laugh with me. Ron doesn't like me. He sort of, what's the word, ignores me. He calls me nuisance, *Hello nuisance*, he says. I don't know why mum lives with him. My real dad wouldn't call me a nuisance. My aunt and uncle don't call me a nuisance. I used to go and stay with them at weekends but mum won't let me to anymore. She said her sister Dot, my aunty, was turning me against her. Just because I said I wish I could live there. Well, I don't care. I do wish I lived there. I wish Aunty Dot was my mum and Uncle Malcolm my dad. Now I wish I'd never said it, then I could still visit. Mum isn't speaking to Aunty Dot. Mum did ask me why. I said because we all played snap and made bread, things like that and Uncle Malcolm had made me a jewellery box for my birthday.

Then the next day after tea mum says, 'I bought some snap cards, we can all play snap', and Ron sighs and we play, mum trying to make it fun and Ron yawning and I couldn't stand it anymore and went up to my room - mum shouting after me to come back, maybe whist would be more...and Ron switching the telly back on.

The next day after tea, mum said she'd bought all the ingredients and should we make some bread together. We did and it was good fun, but this week when I asked her she said she was too busy.

I have to stop now my arm's aching.

February 7^h

I called for my pal Susan today, Saturday. Her mum was still in bed. We had some toast and cranberry juice. It was cool and then we thought about where to go on our bikes, up Tain Hill we decided. On the way up Susan started saying something. I think I can remember how it went.

Susan: Pearl, I want to be blood sisters.
Me: What's that?
Susan: You cut your wrists with a knife and mix up the blood, yours and mine.
Me: Ugh – that sounds horrible!
Susan: I want to tell you a secret, I really want to but I'm feared you'll let it out and I thought if we're sisters, like blood sisters, you wouldn't.
Me: I won't tell Susan, honest.
Susan: I'll only believe you if we're blood sisters.
Me: I hate blood. It makes me want to faint. I did once when my cousin Jenny cut her leg on barbed wire. It was horrible – all the fat cut open.
Susan: This would be a little cut, Pearl, you're just feared.
Me: I'm not.

Susan:	You are.
Me:	Not.
Susan:	Are.
Me:	Not.
Susan:	Do it then.
Me:	Don't have to.
Susan:	Okay then, I'm going back to

Tain.

| Me: | But we're only half way up. |
| Susan: | I don't care, go yourself, |

scaredy cat!

Susan went off down the hill. I didn't want to go on my own – didn't

want to go back to the house and watch telly. I shouted:

'Alright! I'll do it.'

Susan came back panting.

'Good for you. Here we are at the car park. Let's hide our bikes. Come on, Pearl, you're always staring at things. No cars, that's good – we'll have the place to ourselves.'

| Me: | Isn't the firth cool from here? |
| Susan: | Aye, and see Dornoch over |

the way.

| Me: | I'd love to swim over the firth. |
| Susan: | It's too dangerous, there's |

strong currents that would sweep you away.

| Me: | Or a canoe, that would be |

good.

| Susan: | I've got a knife, where would |

be best? In the wood or on top of the hill. There won't be any folk about but perhaps the wood is best, just in case. We'll find a hollow and then seal the pact.

Me: Where did you get the idea?

Susan: From a cowboy film. This Indian and Cowboy became blood brothers. It's an Indian thing I think. Here we are, look we can get down here. Right, no one will see us – come on.

Me: Just hurry and get it over with.

Susan: You've changed your tune.

Me: I want to know the secret.

Susan: Right, here's the knife. I'll cut myself first, ouch! – no blood's coming out again – there, that's better, quick before it dries up, hold out your arm, look at that tree in front...

Me: Ouch!

Susan: Quick – mix the blood.

And a serious voice:

Susan: We are now blood sister and will stay so for ever and ever. We will share secrets but never tell anyone. Death to the sister that does. The pact is sealed.

Me: I don't like the bit about death – did you think to bring any tissues or plasters?

Susan: No, just the knife, sorry – suck it.

Me: Ugh! No.

Susan: It works, honest.

Me: What's the secret?

Susan: You won't tell?

Me: I don't want to die yet! Look my wrist's not stopped bleeding and I've got nothing to put on it.

Susan: Here, I'll rip a bit off my t-shirt, put that around it.

Me: What'll your mum say?

Susan: I'll think of something.

Me: Now tell, Susan – you promised!

Susan: Ok. It's my mum – she drinks, like.

Me: What do you mean?

Susan: '   She drinks whiskey most nights, after tea, watching telly – glass after glass after glass. She gets so drunk that I have to help her upstairs. Then I'm her wee pet, her angel but sometimes she blames me, says it's all my fault, that her life is in a mess. I'm worried, Pearl, worried that she might die. It's horrid seeing her face so red, and she slobbers – it's horrible.

Me: But it doesn't look that red to me – her face, I mean.

Susan: She covers it up with face powder – if anyone's about I mean, apart from me. Then everyday she comes back from work with all these goodies, all my favourites, to make up. I hate it, I hate it. So, I'm not having the food anymore. Well, I have it then I sick it up.

Me: How?

Susan: I put my fingers down my throat – that way I won't grow up. I don't want to be like my mum.

Me: How will that stop it – being sick?

Susan: I saw this programme on telly, bulimic – bulimic something like that – you become so thin you can't have babies – don't want to grow up.

Me: But you have to!

Susan: No you don't, not if you sick your food back.

Me: Isn't it yucky?

Susan: It's pretty horrid but I'm thinner already, look.

Me: Well, yes. Let's go back down I'm hungry, sorry, I didn't think.

Susan: You could do it.

Me: What?

Susan: Sick your food up.

Me: I don't want to.

My wrist stopped bleeding. I told mum I cut it on some glass. She rubbed some Germoline on it and put a plaster on. It hurts a bit but I suppose that's the price you pay for being a blood sister. And this is the most writing I've ever done even though I'm injured! I must be brave!

February 8th

I'm glad I've got a blood sister especially since I saw Aunt Dot and my cousins Jenny and Shona at the shop. I'd gone to get some bread for mum and they were there. I hadn't seen them for ages. Aunt Dot gave me a hug and bought me some crisps and said she was sorry. I couldn't stop crying and went up to my room when I got back, after putting the bread in the bread bin. So, I might have lost Aunt Dot but I've got a blood sister. Aunt Dot makes lovely pictures with dried flowers. She grows the flowers and I sometimes help her pick them, then she puts them in glycerine and water so that they keep their colour – it's very interesting. My mum doesn't know anything about flowers. Our garden is just grass. I asked mum why she didn't grow flowers. She said she didn't have time what with working at the shop and keeping the house tidy. She works at the paper shop part-time. She's always saying there's no money in Aunty Dot's pictures. She says we live better. I have more clothes and shoes, I look a lot smarter than my cousins Jenny and Shona.

I don't know; it seems to me they are a lot happier. I'm only eleven and I don't know anything, mum says. I keep thinking about Susan, I put my fingers down my throat. It was yuk – I don't know how she can do it.

February 10th

It snowed yesterday, enough to go sledging. Susan and me went down the Links. It was great fun. I would have stayed longer but Susan was cold. I asked her if she was still doing it, being sick. She said yes. We sometimes have a race up Castle Brae on the way back but she was too tired.

On Monday mum's cousin Maggie came round with Justin – he's one year old. Cousin Maggie always makes me take him to the Links and gives me money for sweeties. Cousin Maggie's by herself. Her man dumped her, she says. I don't know why. She's a lot prettier than mum. She's got long, blond hair and wears tight jeans. I took Justin to the Links. He's sweet really, but then as I was lifting him out of his pushchair he smelt awful. He'd done a poo. I took him back home but mum and Maggie weren't very pleased to see me. Maggie changed Justin and said, *Off you go*. I said I didn't want to. Mum said I was selfish. I should be glad to give Maggie a break. I said if she was that bothered she should go herself – so she boxed my ears and said I was too cheeky by half. Then I heard her going on to Maggie about how it was Aunt Dot's fault. It isn't Aunt Dot's fault. I don't see why I should take Justin again if I don't want to. He's not even my brother, he's a second cousin. I do like him fine, except when he's got a smelly nappy. What will I do when I'm a mum? Susan won't be a mum.

February 11th

I went to Tain Hill after school today. The snow is all dirty in town but up there it's pure and white. I called for Susan but she didn't want to go. She was watching telly. I sledged down the fields with the Dornoch Firth stretched out, deep blue beyond all the whiteness. I hope it snows again. When I came back I asked mum if she fancied making a snowman, and we did, with her pink scarf and old felt hat. I felt great and then mum asked me how I fancied living in Cromarty. Ron wants to move there she says.

Mum: It would be quite exciting – like an adventure.

Me: What? And leave school and all my mates? Susan is my best pal, I can't!

Mum: We might have to, Pearl, and that's that. Ron seems set on it; he's got relatives there.

Me: Well, all our relatives are here and there's two of us.

Mum: Look Pearl, Ron brings in good money working at Nigg and what he wants counts too.

Me: Why should it matter to me what he wants? He doesn't even notice me.

Mum: Now Pearl, Ron's been good to you. Look at that new coloured telly you've got in your room.

Me: I can't stand him! He stinks.

Mum: 'won't have you speaking that way about Ron, young lady. Go to your room.

Me: Sure! I almost live there anyway, and I won't move to Cromarty, so there!'

(Door bangs.)

God, it's awful. God please help me. I

don't want to move. It took me ages to find Susan. I'll never have a friend like her and if I did make a pal we wouldn't be blood sisters. I'd be in another bedroom, without any pals, forever. I lost Aunt Dot and Uncle Malcolm, Jenny and Shona. Now I'll lose everyone. It's not fair! I don't want to leave. It's all Ron's fault. I wish mum and me were back in the *but and ben,* just the two of us. Mum hasn't had much time for me since then, and that pig doesn't notice me. I could be dead for all he cares. He maybe wishes I were dead.

I'm not going. They've spoilt the snow. I don't care about anything. I've just been to the toilet and been sick. It was horrible but I won't go.

February 13ᵗʰ

I went round to Susan's after school. Her mum wasn't back from work yet – we had some fruit juice.

Me: You know what?
Susan: What?
Me: Mum told me yesterday we might be moving to Cromarty.
Susan: When?
Me: I don't care when. I'm not going.
Susan: Why, why are you moving?
Me: Ron wants to move – I hate him.

121

Susan: What about school?

Me: That doesn't matter does it?

Susan: Of course it matters. Learning matters – it opens doors.

Me: It doesn't matter that much to mum. She never helps me with my projects. She's too busy weighing herself and putting on face creams and having her hair done all the time. It must be for Ron. I can't think why, he's vile and fat. He sits watching videos all night and drinking beer. I'm not allowed to watch the videos. I'm too young. I'm always in my room. That's why I got the coloured telly to keep me out of the way. Susan, I couldn't stand it moving to Cromarty.

Susan: It sounds awful, like my life. You never told me when I told you about mum drinking.

Me: I'm telling you now. I hate Ron and he doesn't like me. I wonder if I was different. I don't know, really pretty like Laura McKay, if he'd notice me then – or if I wasn't so quiet.

Susan: What are you going to do?'

Me: I'm being sick like you. I'd rather die than go to Cromarty.

Susan: Wonder how long it will take before my mum notices how thin I am. Look, I have to fasten up my trousers with safety pins.

Me: How long have you been doing it for?'

Susan: Since the New Year, not properly though. Sometimes I couldn't face it, but I'm getting better.

Me: It's yuk! I'm not going to Cromarty though. It's like I'd have nothing left. I love Tain, it's my home.

Susan: When my mum notices and I tell her, I'm going to say I'll give it all up if she gives up drink.

Me: And I'll give it up if I can stay in Tain.

Susan: It's one way, Pearl. I've thought of running away but they bring you back and it's too cold anyway.

Me: If this doesn't work, maybe we could run away in the Easter Holidays?

Susan: Sure. I'm glad I've got a blood sister.

Me: So am I.

February 14th - Friday

Susan collapsed at school today. They had to bring her mother from work. I heard words like *dangerously thin* and all that. I've been sick. I had to lie on my bed. I wish I was happy. I wish my life were different. I wish I was five. I wish my mum loved me like Aunt Dot does. I wish, I wish, I wish. On the star I can see from my bedroom window.

July 8th

It's lovely and sunny. Susan's mum took the pledge and we didn't move to

Cromarty. I even get to see my Aunt Dot again. Susan and me are going to Guide camp. I can't wait. We have decided to be fit and strong now. It's much better!

A Brief Encounter

By Pam Rowe

John Mackintosh made his way to the Imperial Hotel. He was a trainee journalist with a local paper called *The Cotswold Journal*. His assignment this morning was to interview Martina Stravosky, who was a top ballerina with the Russian Ballet at present performing in Bristol.

He entered the hotel through a revolving circular door and was aware of the opulent setting with its bright red plush carpet and ornate decoration making everything look expensive.

He spoke to the commissionaire in the foyer who suggested he had a word with the concierge, so he made his way over to the reception desk and announced he had an interview booked with Martina. He was then escorted to the lift and taken to the seventh floor where the Penthouse Suite was situated. On arrival he was dismayed to find that he wasn't the only reporter there, so he found a seat and waited. His turn soon came and he was ushered into a private sitting room where a petite beauty was sitting on a sofa surrounded by vases of beautiful flowers. He had never seen anything so breath-taking and he was told he had five minutes to obtain a story before leaving.

After the interview, he left thoroughly disappointed that he had not been better prepared for the experience he had just encountered. He realised that his editor had sent him to the Imperial as a learning curve to widen his knowledge that journalism could be a stimulating but frustrating experience. He had not been able to achieve enough information to write a gripping article about the star and was afraid to return to the office and admit defeat, so decided instead to stroll down to the local riverside and reflect on the disappointing morning.

A couple of hours later he was still gazing into space having tried to save the day by writing a small piece on the information he had managed to obtain. He glanced up as a figure walked by, only to recognise Martina who smiled and asked if she could join him on the seat, which of course he agreed to immediately. She sat down wearily, and he stayed silent whilst she regained composure and, after a few minutes, she turned and smiled at him saying:

'Didn't I meet you earlier at the hotel?

'Yes,' he answered. 'I was one of the many people who wanted to meet you.'

She sighed and said, 'I find it all so exhausting. My life isn't my own anymore. As soon as the interviews and appointments are over I have to rush to the theatre to prepare for my performance, in whatever is the current ballet. Tonight, for instance, it's Coppelia. And by the time I get home it's bed time, and the whole routine is repeated the following day.'

'Don't you ever get any free time?' John asked.

'Only tiny opportunities that I can steal, like this one.'

'That's terrible!' John replied tenderly, very aware of this young woman's stress and unhappiness. Who would have thought that a very successful young star could be so miserable? He decided to offer a friendly ear and help make her life a little more tolerable.

'Why don't you join me for a meal at a country pub that I like? I'm sure you'd feel better with a little food inside your stomach.'

To his delight and surprise she agreed, and they left the seat and made their way along the riverbank to his car.

After about twenty minutes the city was left behind and the countryside opened up to portray rolling hills and colourful meadows and grassy fields, where the only company they had were a few cows and sheep dotted across the landscape. John stopped his car outside a very picturesque country pub and helped Martina out. They entered the building together and found a table in the corner of the bar where they would not be disturbed. They ordered lunch and then sat there chatting about their very different lives, hers in Russia and his in England. She talked about her family back home and how she missed them and told him that she longed to be the girl that only a couple of years ago was full of enthusiasm about becoming the famous ballerina she was today.

All too soon she glanced at her watch.

'I am sorry, John, but we must go. I'm at the theatre in an hour.'

They both left the pub, after John had paid for the meal, and made their way back to the hotel.

John was reluctant to end the day with Martina so, as she was about to leave the car, he suggested he wait for her and take her to the theatre. She agreed readily and before long she had gathered her belongings from her suite and had John again. He smiled and started the car and began their journey to the Bristol theatre ready for her performance. As they arrived she offered him tickets for her private box for the evening performance and then made her way to her dressing room.

John phoned his sister and brother-in-law and asked them if they would like to join him to see the ballet.

Later that day they met him at the theatre entrance, made their way to the auditorium and entered the box, where they settled comfortably and watched with awe this graceful creature delicately gliding across the stage making this popular ballet come alive.

At the end, the whole audience applauded and would not leave until there had been several encores.

John said his goodbyes to his sister but could not bring himself to leave the theatre before seeing Martina once more.

He made his way to her dressing room and knocked on the door and was greeted by her personal dresser who ushered him into the room. Martina, by this time, was ready to leave. He thanked her for the tickets and suggested they found somewhere for a light supper before calling an end to the day.

They found a small intimate restaurant not far from the theatre and again sat together at a table hidden in an alcove. Although Martina looked tired she soon began to relax and ordered a chicken dish followed by a fruity sweet and a coffee. John ordered the same. During the meal they engaged in a light conversation and realised they both had similar views and interests.

After the meal was over John took Martina back to the hotel and they said their goodbyes, as the ballet company was leaving in the morning for another venue in the United Kingdom.

The next morning, John submitted the article – written the night before - to his mentor and editor. It was received by his boss, who was greatly surprised and delighted at his student's efforts and the standard of reporting he'd achieved.

After leaving the editor's office John was greeted by a fellow reporter who had an envelope in his hand.

'While you were in with the Boss, this was delivered to reception for you.'

John sat at his desk opening the package with anticipation: it contained a brochure of future engagements of the touring Russian Ballet, plus a small notelet containing Martina's mobile telephone number.

John was amazed and happy at the thought of the possibility of seeing Martina again.

He sat at his desk for a little while, dreaming of what the future could hold and hoping their brief encounter would develop into a love affair so that he could protect this young, gorgeous, unhappy ballerina from the mundane monotonous existence of her current life.

He picked up the telephone, dialled the number on the notelet and, as Martina answered, he said:

'John here...'

Easter Assignment

By Kenneth Blyth

For our assignment over the Easter holidays our writers were given a table with various lines of poetry, words and objects in them and asked to choose one from each and incorporate them into a story. This is what Kenneth came up with, using his choices with great imagination and flare.

Table 1: June is a cruel month, the scoriaceous sun consumes my wings in a flash
Travelling through the green sky with a desperate cry
Table 2: Bird, Fox, Heard
Table 3: An Old German board game – Philopena – played with nuts...

~

The sky looked green through my visor, the June sun blazing. From my camp on the cliff side I could see all the way down the valley - covered by ancient trees and the dark clouds over head.
I had to escape.
I heard a voice through my com system,

but the approaching clouds were disrupting the signal.

Damn it, I said to myself, replacing the battery pack in my suit, making a quick prayer - and then I jumped, abandoning all my belongings. My suit's flight systems should be kicking in but weren't - I could feel the wing membranes trying to deploy but something was stopping them and I was plummeting fast towards the tree canopy.

'Martin, what's happening?' I called, trying to stop myself from panicking. A small purple orb floated in front of my visor.

'There isn't enough power, Sir,' the AI answered, unphased by the fact that we were both about to die – we shared the same body, after all, at least the machinery parts, and he was the closest thing I had to a friend.

'Divert power from life systems and sensors!' I ordered.

'Sir, you'll be near blind and freezing,' Martin stated passively, as was his way.

'Just do it! I can use my eyes!' I shouted.

'Very well,' Martin complied immediately, the temperature suddenly dropping and my visor's HUD disappearing, but finally I could feel the wings deploying: four metres length of thin blue membranes, and the means by which I could control my descent. The small thrusters of my suit fired up too and I was able to make a swoop over the forest canopy moments before I crashed.

Hovering just above the trees, I took my

bearings.

The clouds were starting to loom over me, the wind was picking up.

'Martin, how long can we fly?' I asked.

'Seventeen minutes,' he said.

'Just enough.' I breathed, relieved, and turned for home, when a streak of green lightning suddenly flashed to my left and struck the ground, and from the point of impact arose a form: a woman, wearing chain of armour over a white robe, and with a pair of large, ethereal gold wings like a bird's stretching from her back. She looked straight at me, though her eyes were covered by a metallic visor like my own.

My fear and panic was immediate and intense.

'Martin,' I gulped. 'I need all the speed you can give me.'

'Agreed.' the orb responded, and the thrusters strained as he managed to increase the power and I accelerated out of the valley, the ground beneath me nothing but a blur, my face freezing, despite the visor.

'The Huntresses are out early today.' Martin commented.

'Too early,' I agreed. 'We've got to get home and warn the others. Are we far enough to send a clear signal?' I inquired.

'Signal is still being disrupted,' came Martin's calm voice, 'but not by the clouds.'

Ah Shit, I whispered, then saw the light in my visor darken slightly and suddenly banked myself to my right, a crimson bolt of energy narrowly missing my wing. Turning my head I saw the huntress flying near me, a small smirk on her face, an energy pistol in one hand, a lance in the other.

'Don't suppose we've any weapons?' I asked Martin, trying not to give any sign of fear to opponent.

'You left them at the camp,' came Martin's reply.

Of course I did, cursing my initial panic that had made me jump so precipitously when I first saw the clouds. No help for it now. I lowered myself down so I just a few meters above the ground.

'You do have some nuts and kernels in your right pocket,' the orb stated, presumably meaning the game counters might serve as weapons.

'Maybe I should ask her for a game of Philopena,' I joked. The AI didn't respond, humour not Martin's strong point. Either way, I didn't chance a chance in the open, so I made a decision, headed towards a small opening in the forest. For a brief second I heard a distorted voice coming through my coms and Martin's orb blinked, but soon as I landed in the shrubbery it was gone.

'Cut the power, Martin,' and Martin did, engines going off line, wings retracting, me running into a denser part of the forest so the Huntress couldn't swoop down on me from above. After a few minutes I stopped to catch my breath, hiding in a small recess beneath a tree, sitting up and listening for any sign of my pursuer – but there was nothing except the rustle of the wind in the trees and the birds singing.

'Martin, I need sensors again,' I whispered

'I wouldn't recommend that, Sir,' he advised. 'It's likely she can track your suit's power signature.'

He was right. So I retracted my visor, my eyes suddenly awash with colour so it took me a couple of blinks for my vision to return to normal and, looking, saw her silhouetted through the canopy.

I froze, thinking this was it, but she slowly flew on.

At least something's gone my way, I thought, and carefully picked myself up and moved deeper into the woods. A short while later, I was moving parallel to a river, sticking close enough to the woods that I wouldn't be exposed - but I was gasping for a drink. I glanced up, but could see no sign of her and decided to take a chance. Immediately the wind started streaking through the trees so it sounded like the whole forest was screaming, and there was that same distortion once more through my coms.

'What the hell is that, Martin?' I shouted over the wind.

No response, and the purple orb was blank.

'Martin! Martin!' I shouted again, panic rising through my bones.

'Sorry...Gabriel...' Martin's voice, weak, faltering. 'I tried to.. fight it... but I've... failed you.'

His orb shifted shades as the timbre of his voice dropped, changing to a deep dark red so he looked like a scoriaceous sun. And then he drained all the remaining power in my suit and fried my flight control, made my wings were useless. A wave of anger rushed over me, for this was effectively my death warrant. Then the wind went crazy again, picked up and threw me across the forest floor, sending me into a rock with an audible crack and splinter of bone. I winced in pain, tried to move, but my body refused.

I looked up again and saw the clouds dissipating and scattering, revealing a huge shape in the centre like a massive bird of prey silhouetted against the sun, wings so huge I couldn't see then from end to end – and just like those of the Huntress. The hairs went up all over my body and there she was: the Huntress emerging from behind a tree carrying her gun. Some loose leaves clung to her armour, same expression on her face as before as she extended her free hand and there went Martin's orb towards her - up and over, circling her hand.

I tried to get up, but with Martin in her control and with no power I couldn't move. Instead I started at her intently, doing my best to look defiant.

'At least make it quick,' I growled, as she approached, standing just a few feet from me so

I could see her fox-coloured hair going down into her collar, and I could smell the scent of rosemary.

She laughed, a beautiful melodious sound, quite at odds with the mockery evident on her face. She pointed above me at the huge, looming ship as a beam of light appeared from its bow and up went Martin's orb to greet it.

And then I understood.

It was never me she was interested in but him.

To her I was just a bag of useless meat and augments.

She held her gun at my head and fired.

Blues for Morag

By Josephine S. J. Sumner

Morag was ironing. There was a huge pile still waiting accusingly. Her six year old son was jumping off the settee and rolling over.

'Not too rough, now', said Morag looking up from a blue shirt sleeve.

Her son, Ross, jumped a few more times and then came up to his mum at the ironing board.

'Can we go to the swing park?' he said.

'Not today, Ross, it's wet and I have all this ironing to do'.

'I want to go to the swing park', he persisted.

'I'm not going in the rain. I took you yesterday. Find something else to do'

'What?'

'You could watch telly'.

'I'm fed up with telly'.

'You could draw or paint'.

'No, I don't want to'.

'Make something with your lego'.

'I want to go to the swing park', he whined.

'Don't whine, Ross. I'm not going and that's it'.

'Can I go on my own then?'

'No, you cannot go on your own. You

are not old enough yet and there are too many busy roads'.

'It's not fair, other boys go on their own'.

'I don't care what other boys do, Ross, they're probably older or have more road sense, you forget where you are and don't look out for cars'.

'I do, I do – I want to go'.

'Well, you're not going, final'.

Ross went into the sitting room and slumped on the settee in a pique.

Morag carried on with her ironing and sighed. It was hard sometimes, him being an only child and his dad gone. She did try to keep him amused. Today though, she wanted the ironing out of the way, not starting it at nine o'clock when Ross was in bed. She had the shop tomorrow and it would be good to read Ross his story and then come downstairs and relax for a couple of hours. She'd ignore Ross and he'd come out of it. Probably it was one of those days when everything felt awkward, not right and him jammed in the middle of it – making it worse. She had days like that herself but she had to make a stand sometimes or else he'd see his mum as a pushover. She very nearly was anyway. Sometimes she felt she overcompensated by being both a mum and dad to the boy. She didn't want him to miss out.

The rain fell steadily. Morag laid down her iron and put more coal on the fire. She always did this if it was raining. The brighter the fire burned, the more it warmly contrasted the grey and damp. Her eyes locked with Ross's over the room.

'Can I have a shot of that guitar?'

'What guitar?'

'The one locked away in that cupboard under the stairs'.

'No, Ross'.

'Why?'

'I don't want you to play the guitar'.

Why?'

'I don't think any good comes from it?'

'How do you know?'

'I think it makes people irresponsible, makes them forget about people they should be looking after'.

'But I'm not 'people', mum – I'm Ross – let me have a shot'.

'Why Ross?'

'Dad showed me a few chords, remember? Please mum'.

'Oh, Ross, you don't give up do you. I'd rather you didn't'.

'There's nothing else to do. I'm fed up and I want to try something new and you won't let me. It's not fair'. Ross burst into tears.

'I won't let you because it took your dad away from us', said Morag coldly and firmly.

'What did?'

'His guitar, his music, his band...'

'But it's not my fault, mum'.

'I know its not your fault'.

'I'm not dad'.

'I know son, but you might be the same'.

'I want to play the guitar, mum, I want to make music. It seems like a magic thing to do'. His eyes shone at the thought.

Morag saw the brightness of his eyes. When had she last seen it? At the Christmas concert. Him only five years old and chosen to sing a carol, 'Little Donkey'. He sang with a sureness and purity that was amazing. When he came to her at the end of the concert his eyes were glowing like stars and she'd squashed him hadn't she.

'That's the last time you go shaming us like that, what an idiot you looked'. The light had gone. *'You can't keep on doing that'* said a voice in her head. *'Putting out that light, that brightness, that proud look. You can't keep on punishing him for his dad's desertion. You can't stop a natural talent because of resentment'.*

Morag took a deep breath and looked at Ross.

'Yes, you can have a shot of the guitar'.

'Oh mum, thanks' and he gave her a hug. He wasn't very demonstrative and Morag savoured the spontaneous warmth.

'Let's get the key'.

The cupboard was opened. It was like a floodgate to the swamp of memories she'd blocked out.

Ross sat on the sofa with the old Yamaha acoustic still with all the strings attached badly in need of tuning. He had on his face that look his dad had, dreamy yet intent, away to another place. He similarity was startling. The same curly black hair, green eyes, full lips and expression on his face.

Morag sighed softly and went back to her ironing in the kitchen section of the large room. She looked up at the flames dancing on the fire and saw when she'd met Ross's dad, Jamie, in that house down by the sea. He'd taken out his guitar, the one Ross was plucking and played and sang with something that quietened the folk. It was as if he took you to another place. Yet the sea was there and the mountains, heather, golden light and warmth. It was hard to put it into words it was more a feeling, a really good feeling. She was smitten. Maybe he could see it in her eyes because he came over to where she was sitting by the window and introduced himself.

Ross was singing now. He looked over to see if she approved and she smiled. He had the gift like his dad.

Jamie and herself were inseparable after that - lots of fun, lots of love, lots of laughter and tenderness. She was working in the newsagents, didn't really have a talent like Jamie but looking back she supposed she'd been pretty and young and vibrant and read books. They were in love and she went to Jamie's gigs and they walked and swam and drank, skated on ice, went to the cinema, kissed and cuddled and chatted and stroked. It was like they existed in Jamie' golden land he created with his music. The music started to take off and Jamie got himself an agent. They electrified the band and to her mind something was lost but not as far as the band was concerned. Jamie said their love spurred him on, gave him confidence.

Then she became pregnant and Jamie was delighted. They married straight away at the Registry Office. It was a lovely day in April with the yellow of the spring flowers and the sun was shining. All around them everything was re-awakening and she with her new life in her. Jamie had sung a song he'd written for her, full of his love and she'd sat blooming amongst the crowd of folk, bonny and glad.

They'd rented a cottage in the centre of town, this one. All their family and friends had given them furniture. It was always full of folk. She'd gradually got bigger and Jamie's band was touring all over Scotland. Eventually she'd stopped going to the gigs. There were more and more rehearsals at the house as Jamie was a perfectionist. She cooked and cleaned and made coffee and tea and tried to smooth things and latterly tried not to mind that Jamie was frequently away. He wanted to make good money he said for her and the baby.

The band were support for a big named group in Inverness and offered a single tour of America if that went down well. It was in a blue and white striped marquee, her pal Trish had told her when she came round that Saturday afternoon. Trish went out with Barry the base player in Jamie's band.

'Isn't Jamie home yet?'

'No, Trish, I'm worried about him'.

'I wouldn't worry, he's alright'.

'How do you know?'

'He seemed well enough when I last saw him'.

'When was that?'

'At the end of the gig'.

'Have you seen any of the band since then?'

'Barry, that's all'.

'Why hasn't he phoned, Trish?'

'Maybe he's busy'.

'It's not like him', said Morag. 'I should phone the police'.

'I wouldn't if I were you'.

'I can't stop worrying'

'Look, Morag, don't fret, he'll be home soon'.

'I'd best phone the police'.

'Calm down'. Trish's arm went round me. She patted my shoulder.

'Shall I make some tea?'

'Yes please'.

Trish made the tea and it was as if she wanted to say something. Morag put some coal on the fire as it was November and cold.

'What if he's had an accident?'

'I don't think he has, Morag'.

'What makes you so sure. You know something and you're not telling, that's it isn't it? Tell me Trish, you're meant to be my best pal'.

'I'll tell you about the evening then. It's just what I saw, Morag – I mean, I might have ...'

'Don't haver, tell me what you saw'.

'It was a brilliant marquee, blue and white and the lightening effects were great. Jamie's band came on. Barry on base was something else, you know – the pulse of it vibrated straight through me. Your Jamie was excellent and right from the start this female jumped up. She was, well, like a panther, a big cat jumping about. How she could dance. She'd on a bodysuit in red lurex so low at the front that you wondered how her boobs stayed in, she wobbled them about enough. Her total intent was on your Jamie. She was dancing for him whilst everyone watched and listened, she was stunning but what a brass neck she had! Then Jamie came off the stage and grabbed her and they danced together. It was magnetic. They rubbed up against each other, they moved their hands down each other's' bodies, they stared into each other's' eyes. They kissed for a long time and he went back on stage and finished the song. The crowd cheered and cheered'.

A bolt went through Morag.

'You think he's with her?'

'I was with Barry and the rest of the band and we all came home together in Barry's van apart from Jamie. When they were loading the gear into the vans she sort of slinked up and just stood by Jamie's van and Jamie said 'Get in', and they drove off together'.

'That's why you didn't want me to phone the police'.

'Look, Morag, this can happen with bands, it doesn't mean anything. He loves you, you know he does'.

'I can't take it in'.

'Maybe nothing happened anyway. Let him explain first.'

'Do you mind going Trish?'

'Look Morag, I'm sorry I...'

'I want to be alone'.

Morag walked slowly and heavily up to the bedroom and crept into bed and cried.

He came in later. She heard him coming up the stairs, not running up like he usually did after a gig – slowly, dragging his feet. She turned to the bedroom door. He opened it and she could see in his eyes that it was true. He'd been with the panther woman.

'It'll never be the same again', she said and it wasn't

She told her mum about it and she said that these things happened. Some women could turn a blind eye and some couldn't. It depended on the sort of woman you were. Morag didn't know if she could. Jamie said it wouldn't happen again if it upset her so much.

Trish and Morag went to Loch Eye to see the greylag geese. It was frosty, a hoar frost and the sun was going down bathing everything in a pink light and the crescent moon was just coming up. The gaggle of geese pulled at a chord inside Morag. There were thousands of them. She wanted to fly with them. She wanted to fly somewhere where life was easy, not complicated, and her heavy and lumpy with Ross too! She wanted to fly to that golden land which she and Jamie had had but now was lost. Ross stirred inside her and she knew she'd be here for a long time for Ross, no matter what happened.

She heard through the grapevine that panther woman was at some of the local gigs. Jamie said he couldn't ban her from attending could he - he got quite angry.

The band was touring America when Morag had Ross. She'd never known such pain but soon forgot it when they put him in her arms. How she loved that baby and when Jamie came back he was so proud to be a dad. Then he was off on another tour. He was famous and Morag tried to be part of it but she couldn't really, breast feeding Ross. She wanted to be at home. She needed a nest, a lair, a den. They slowly grew apart and when he decided to move to America Morag thought it best to stay. He didn't say much about life on the road and silences were guilt. He couldn't help himself. There would be many panther women. Morag couldn't turn a blind eye anymore.

Morag came back with a start to her

ironing.   Ross was still singing and strumming away in his own fashion. He'd need lessons.

Goodbyes

By Pam Rowe

The countryside had its winter coat on. The trees were bare and showed their shapes prominently as the branches were covered in white frost instead of leaves. The ground beneath them was hard and white and the whole area signified a cold and unfriendly place. This was added to, as the piece of land had been put aside as a burial ground for war victims killed in the trenches during the First World War.

Silas Smith was an officer of the First Battalion Regiment, about to go home to his family, and had decided to take one last look at the place that had been his posting for many months - leading to days of uncertainty, dodging bullets in rat-infested trenches filled with slimy mud and the smell of death. He remembered all the men that he had known while in charge of the action and thought of them with affection, and part of his fold as he would or did of his family back home. The men he was about to leave in this dismal place had been mere boys, terribly afraid of what life would bring and also homesick for the life they had left behind, never to return, all with different personalities and needs which he had tried to understand and support, even though he was   busy with the manoeuvres of war.

He looked around him now at the desolation of the sight, with its squalid memories very much in his mind, taking note of the tarpaulin sheets and the corrugated iron that lay about reminding him of former battles. Stones lay about the area, all used to cover graves of the men that had died, all of whom Silas had known personally. He was very aware of a large stone slab in front of him that was glistening in the sun and made the shadow of his body more prominent on the stone. The scene made the last four years even more significant to him, of the horror that had come and passed, and how he hoped it could become a place of peace and tranquillity for the soldiers to rest and be made more beautiful for people coming to the area to revisit their loved ones in the future.

He walked away, knowing he was going home to be embraced by his family and to re-kindle his old life back in England knowing he would see it in all its glory of the Spring countryside, with trees coming into blossom complimenting the new fresh green of the young leaves, and would watch the daffodils popping through after the snowdrops had finished flowering, cowslips would follow - being a great favourite of his wife. He was one of the lucky ones. God had spared him, and he made a vow at this time that the life he had been given would not be wasted.

The Nativity Play

By Bryan Rowe

Task: to write a script for the opening sequence of a play and leave off at a point ehre the reader would want to see what would happen next...

Setting:

A village hall, where the local drama group is to present a modern version of the Nativity Story.

Chris Dyke, the writer/director, wants to stage a very modern take on the story with some audience participation.

Opening Scene:

We see three characters gathered around the stage area of the hall:

Chris Dyke Director
Marie   Producer
Griff   General
Assistant/Props/administrator

The three are meeting before members of the cast arrive for the group's first read-through of the script, and to share ideas for the overall production.

Chris is sitting on the edge of the stage shuffling through pages of the script. He is wearing a sloppy polo neck jumper and a pair of bleached blue jeans.

Marie is standing just to the left of him, deep in contemplation, staring at the back of the hall. She is dressed in a black loose shirt and tight black jeans. She wears glasses.

Griff is sitting in a chair facing Chris. He is an active member of the local Golf Club and is always tuned into local gossip and news. He is dressed in a white jumper and tartan trousers, and has been playing golf that afternoon.

The play begins:
Chris puts the script down by the side of him.

Chris: Right then. Let's have a quick resumé of where we are at in terms of casting and production issues

Marie: I've received several replies from my emails regarding requests for help with the production, which are very encouraging. *Get There* - the Sat Nav company - are willing to let us use their name in exchange for a half page advertising slot in the programme. They liked the idea of the *Three Wise Guys* being guided to the hall to enable them to bid for the signed autographed photo of Madonna that's going to be auctioned at the close of the first night's performance

Chris: I was dead lucky to get that photo, thanks to my brother-in-law being a recording engineer with her record company

Marie   Bill Stevens has agreed to let

us use his BSA motor bike for Joseph and Mary's entrance. He'll supervise Joseph's handling of the bike as he rides into the hall

Chris: Yes, there are some Health and Safety issues here!

Marie: Dilys, the drama teacher at the Academy, has confirmed that a group of her senior girl students are pleased to be Angels and will perform as a Rock Band. They're calling themselves *The Clipped Wings*

Chris: That will be a great attraction to bring in the parents and other pupils to see the show

Griff has been looking more and more pensive as the conversation between Chris and Marie has progressed. He sits upright in the chair.

Griff: Of course you realise that you are going to have problems tonight. Several members of the cast are not happy with the roles you have given them. Ben has told me he is particularly annoyed, and feels left out,as you have cast him as the Pub Landlord. He sees this as such a minor part. He only has a few lines of dialogue, finishing with the final punch line *Sorry, Pal. We're full!*

Chris: Look Griff, just because Ben fancies himself as a reincarnation of Richard Burton, he's no actor and has a poor stage presence

Marie: Aye, you even had to get him bumped off in the first scene of the murder mystery we put on last year!

Griff becomes more impatient

Griff: OK, but your real problems are going to be over your casting of Mary. Shona Forsyth is really put out that you didn't put her in the Star Role. She's the youngest woman in the company and felt she was made for the part

Chris becomes agitated

Chris: Shona is now well into her late twenties but looks older; she has two kids and definitely hasn't the aura of Mary. She's down to play the role of the Midwife, which will give her the chance to demonstrate compassion at the moment of the birth

Marie   Don't forget, Griff, that Martha Smith has agreed to loan us her baby as the Baby Jesus, which the Midwife - under a spotlight - will lift up from the cot for all the audience to admire. A great moment for Shona!

Chris: Anyway, I have some good news over the casting of Mary. I have been trawling around locally in search of a suitable person to play her and have managed to persuade young Aileen Grant who works at the *Top Knot* hairdressers to take the part. She's single, attractive, and will make a great Mary. She has done some acting with the Academy Drama group when she was a pupil there

Griff: I'm just warning you, Chris. You may have quite a confrontation on your hands with Shona at tonight's meeting

Griff has only just stopped speaking when Shona walks into the hall looking daggers drawn at Chris.

Disruption – A Novel

By Bryan Rowe

Preface to the novel

The history of Scotland during the first fifty years of the Nineteenth Century is full of dramatic events and changes effecting large numbers of the population, most significantly within the Scottish Highlands. The savage years of the Highland Clearances and the Potato Famine of the 1840's have been well documented. Equally, the stories of large numbers of Highlanders emigrating to Canada and New Zealand illustrated the determination of the people concerned to find new opportunities to live out their Christian faith and bring up their families in a fresh, safe, non-oppressive environment.

The 1843 Disruption was another historic milestone, this time centred on the established Church of Scotland, when over four hundred of its ordained ministers voted to leave the church and form a new Free Church of Scotland. The main reason for this split was over who should have the leading role in selecting a new minister: the Congregation or the Landowner.

The novel tells of the events leading up to and following the Disruption. It follows two

Ministers who have been lifelong friends, but have opposing views over the future of the Church and the challenge facing the minister that votes to leave. The immediate effect of ministers voting to leave the established church was that, overnight, they would immediately lose their Annual Stipends, the use of their Manse, Church Buildings and divided their Congregations.

Chapter 1

It was a bitterly cold late afternoon on the 20th January 1841.Throughout the day thick black clouds had brought in further falls of snow. Rev Angus Munro rode his horse Jonah at a gentle trot along a rough snowbound track as straight as a die. With the impending gloom he could just see enough to follow the way ahead to the village of Marnoch in the Presbytery of Strathbogie. He was a man of slight build, the long thick black coat he was wearing with a woollen scarf wrapped around his neck and layers of woollen garments underneath, gave the perspective of a stead and his rider perfectly matched. The large saddle bags draping the saddle contained his personal items, the remains of a piece his wife Mary had prepared for him and his large black leather bound bible he had cherished throughout the thirty years of his ministry. Given to him by his Mother and Father. Angus was so used to riding Jonah in all weathers throughout his large rural parish near Dundee, many days journeying up to twenty miles a day visiting the sick and housebound and preaching at other churches under his watch.

The cold north wind heralded another flurry of fresh snow ,Angus could just make out the outcrop of rocks jutting out on the strathy; the winding outline of the River Logie ahead seemed to defy the falling darkness. On the morrow he will be attending the Marnoch church to join an assembly of parishioners for a meeting that will lead to a divisive step being taken that will change the complete direction of his beloved Church of Scotland. Increasingly under the system of Patronage the selection or *call* of a new minister to a church had been taken out of the hands of the congregation and often a completely unsuitable cleric was foisted upon them by a local land owner or dignity.

Jonah's hoofs hit a large area of frozen ice that cracked underneath their weight and seemed to Angus to be a sign to him that his church was at breaking point. The cold then seemed to pierce through to every bone in his body. The track gave way to a wider road and he could see the lights from some cottage windows ahead. He gave a sigh of relief, his long journey's end was in sight.

As he drew closer to the village he could see smoke rising from the chimneys that echoed the warmth of peat fires; a reminder to him of his own manse and tea by the fireside with Mary.

As he came into the village there seemed to be a large number of wagons and carriages tied up outside well-lit dwellings. He could hear chatter and laughter from within. This suggested people had already travelled from outwith the parish to ensure the severe weather would not deter them from attending the very important meeting.

The manse was situated close to the

church that stood on a hill set in several acres of land, it had been a sacred religious site for many centuries. A gate at the side of the manse, a large grey stone austere looking building, was open, ahead a small barnlike building was lit by a lantern, the floor was covered in fresh straw, Angus tied Jonah to a post and the horse gave a muffled neigh as if to say *at last.*

Angus was to stay with his lifelong friend Rev Murdo King. They had first met at Trinity College Aberdeen to train for the ministry and soon became the best of buddies. Their shared enthusiasm and commitment to their calling they both experienced never faltered.

Murdo had always been particularly attracted to the traditional role of the church in its recognition and authority granted to it by the assembly in Edinburgh, the government and state. The Bible was to him always respected but its interpretation left to the minister and individual to find their own destiny from it. Over the years his ministry had become more entrenched in keeping to the protocol and direction of the churches main assembly. He had never missed the Annual Assembly gathering.

To the contrary, Angus held a firm fundamental evangelical approach to his calling and responsibilities as a minister. His belief and prime concern was to preach Gods revelation in the Bible, through the spirit of Christ and his redemption for the sins of man a person had to experience a conversion and commit themselves to a new life of a complete faith in Christ alone. The other aspect of the minister's role and his obligations to the church and state were to be acknowledged but interpreted through scripture. He had only attended the Annual Assembly twice.

Over the years since their ordination the two had kept closely in touch through letters and mutually arranged family visits. Biblical interpretation remained a constant arena for their arguments and discussions and normally in the end agreeing to differ.

Angus went over to the front door of the manse and gave a forceful rap in the hope his friend would not keep him waiting too long in the cold a minute longer.

He heard Murdo shout, *that's him, he's arrived!*

Chapter 2

A large oil painting depicting Christ serving the wine to the disciples at the Last Supper hung on the middle of the white wall of the manse dining room. An oak dining table stood at the centre covered by a lace tablecloth with three silver holders, each with four candles, placed at either end, reflecting on the silver service laid out for the meal.

As Rosemary, Murdo's wife brought the food in from the kitchen; Murdo poured some of his own red wine into three crystal glasses and passed them round.

'I was given a case of this French red by one of our local merchants after giving some advice on a new business deal he was embarking on,' he said. 'I think you'll enjoy it, Angus.'

Angus sat at the opposite end of the table to Murdo and, in contrast to his friend, who was dressed quite casually, sat tight-bound in a black three quarter length frock coat with two long white linen bands hanging from his collar.

'As usual you're looking very smart in your uniform,' Murdo gibed. 'I've always said they'll put you in your coffin wearing your Geneva Bands'.

'You may jest, Murdo,' Angus replied, 'but you should never forget the reasons behind them. My Geneva Bands, as you call them, still represent the cloven tongues of fire that every minister should hope to be endowed with at his ordination.'

Murdo did not look much chastened, but he didn't want to antagonise further.

'The Immersion of the Holy Spirit, yes,' he replied. 'That was some day when we were ordinated.'

He didn't add how lapsed his own vows had lately become.

Rosemary served ample helpings of lamb stew and vegetables.

'Up to you usual standard,' said Angus

'Och, what else?' she joked. 'And I've made your favourite pudding: Clootie Dumpling.'

She was a tall, round faced woman from Glasgow, with a warm smile, full of confidence. She complimented Murdo as the minister's wife. She enjoyed socialising with the other women in the parish yet was equally competent at protecting her husband from unwelcome callers at the manse. Her cooking made a deep impression on their special visitors, both locally and from Edinburgh.

Angus greatly appreciated when the two families met together. He enjoyed the intimate conversations he shared with Murdo on the theological and political developments within the church. He especially found refreshing his friend's wit and sense of humour.

After saying Grace before the meal, Murdo recalled the occasion when one of his minister friends was returning from the mission field in India; it had been a particularly stormy night and the ship was listing from side to side. His friend pronounced the Grace by saying:

For what we are about to receive, O Lord, Make us truly thankful, bur please give us Your Grace to help us retrieve it.

During the main course of the supper, conversation centred around an exchange of the latest family news, Angus wondered, however, when the subject of the special induction service taking place the next day would be mentioned, and also what Murdo's own reaction would be to his current suspension from all his ministerial duties locally.

It seemed to Angus that his friend's calling had gone adrift.

As Rosemary served the clootie dumpling, Murdo suddenly announced:

'We've got some good news for you, Angus.'

Quite perplexed by this statement Angus replied:

'I cannot imagine how this can be, as here you are now - suspended from your preaching and parochial duties within this parish. Good news? God does move in a most mysterious way.'

'Well, Angus, as you know I have many friends within high places in Edinburgh and, if my appeal against my suspension is successful, I have been offered a position working in the church's Central Administration. There will be a variety of duties, some oversight of the church's Mission Programme and assisting in the organising and planning of the Annual Assembly, which of course you never attend. Our two daughters are now both living in Edinburgh so we both feel the opening could be heaven sent.'

'You just cannot be sure your appeal will be successful,' insisted Angus. And if it's not, then what?'

'Don't worry! I have complete faith that sense will prevail,' he replied.

Rosemary sensed a tension building up between the two men and firmly stated:

'You two will have plenty to talk about later; so Angus, tell us more about how your son John is enjoying his position in Banking in Edinburgh.'

As Angus spoke about his son's progress, Murdo also reflected on the different paths their friendship had taken. Angus had been a real stalwart, having served in just the one parish for nearly thirty years; he had established a *tight ship* and, with the support of five loyal elders, he seemed to be completely immersed within the boundaries of his parish. Murdo enjoyed eavesdropping on this very secure - but to him, very limited - way of serving God. Having ministered in three different parishes himself, he strived for wider horizons. He enjoyed the status a minister's role afforded him and the chances to make full use of the network of his friends within the moderate section of the church. He saw the power that government and state could use to embellish the direction of the church. He was equally at home hobnobbing with the local dignitaries, merchants or land owners with whom he came into contact with each day. He viewed the current crisis as a stepping-stone to more proactive opportunities within the church.

Angus thanked Rosemary for such an appetising and enjoyable meal.

'Home cooking at its best,' he said.

Murdo poured himself a glass of the best malt whisky from the sideboard, knowing that this was one spirit his friend would never partake in.

'Let's go through to the study,' he suggested. 'We need a chance to iron out any misunderstandings that may have arisen between us.'

The study, a small room that seemed to be more enclosed by the full shelves of books completely lining two walls, a large oak writing desk with an oil lamp on top, together with a crackling log fire and two high winged back chairs set the scene for a confrontation that both men knew was inevitable.

'You seem very complacent about your suspension order,' Angus commented, sipping at his almost depleted glass of wine. 'I was shocked to hear about it. How many other ministers from this presbytery have been suspended?'

'Seven of us altogether,' Murdo replied.

'No longer able to preach or fulfil the duties in this parish... What on earth possessed you to agree with the decision of the Civil

Courts when they overruled the authority of our church in the appointment of Mr Edwards?' Angus went on, leaning forward, trying to understand. 'Did it not occur to you what would happen if you kept pushing Mr Edwards forward on the parish? A man the congregation have no liking for at all.'

'Mr Edwards is a perfectly respectable choice for a nominee minister,' Murdo began to defend himself, cut off by Angus snorting loudly.

'I'm beginning to think you deserved the church's punishment,' he said, staring hard at his friend's face.

'Now listen, Angus,' Murdo insisted, 'as true ministers of the Church of Scotland we have to honour and respect the decisions of the Civil Courts of our land who, in their wisdom, judged it right that Mr Edwards should become minister of this church under the official patronage laws. We rely so much on our patrons to finance much of our church's work, especially the development of education in our church schools.'

At this stage Angus was becoming more impatient with his friend's legal stance.

'But what about the wishes of the congregation?' he pleaded. 'This conflict over Mr Edwards has now dragged on for nearly four years! When he was initially presented by a certain land owner, out of three hundred heads of families only one person supported his call and that person was the local innkeeper. Does that not tell you something about his social connections?'

Murdo sighed and took a deep breath, and another swallow of whisky to give him some space to respond to this line of attack. He cleared his throat and stared at the fire.

'Our church here is just one of many parishes throughout Scotland and this in no way sets a precedence. Look at your own situation, Angus,' he said, moving his glance back from the fire. 'Your own position is secure as a rock, both now and in the future.'

'Yes,' snapped Angus, 'but God only knows what might happen in years to come when I'm no longer around. No, there has to be no more State interference with our church,' he continued to argue. 'Have you already forgotten the similar crisis that arose in Auchterader? The Lord Kinoul presented a Mr Robert Young to be the new minister, and out of three thousand souls only two individuals, *two individuals,* Murdo, supported the call. Yet following the Court's decision Mr Young was nevertheless appointed.'

Angus leaned forward before going on.

'No, my friend. I'm afraid we are facing a very cold wind of change in our church's history. There can be no new meaning to the gospel message the church must be proclaiming. I tell you, there is a spiritual awakening and revival moving across the Highlands, and one where the Spirit of our Lord will direct us in deciding the appointment of our ministers.'

Murdo smiled back at his friend expecting Angus to continue, which Angus did.

'Tell me Murdo, when Mr Edwards attends the church tomorrow for his induction service how many people do you expect to attend or choose to stay away?'

Angus walked out of the manse the next day alone.

Murdo had decided to exclude himself from any form of participation in the ordinance proceedings which were now less than an hour away; he expected visits from some of the other suspended ministers and knew that Angus would give him a detailed account of the day.

Chill winds overnight had drifted further falls of snow which now lay deep in high banks against the roadside. Angus felt strangely alone, the uncertainty of the day ahead bore heavily upon him. He seemed to be moving further away from his comfort zone, events were overtaking themselves. The conversation the two men argued over last evening had strayed well past midnight, Murdo seemed to be moving further toward a secular approach rather than acknowledging it is the Holy Spirit that must be the church's guide.

Angus carried his bible under his arm; as he turned to walk towards the church his steps faltered on the icy path but he regained his balance and put his best foot forward.

He was astonished to see dozens of

people walking towards the church, a very large crowd gathered around the church gate. There was a low murmur of conversation, most stood in quiet contemplation. Some children moved and fidgeted between the folds of their mother's tartan-lined cloaks either becoming impatient or feeling the extreme cold. People also lined the path to the main door of the church, two or three deep. As Angus made his way up the path some onlookers bowed their heads with respect as he passed them, acknowledging his status, sensing he was a minister who was attending the service.

He reached the main entrance of the church and out of the crowd a middle aged, heavily-built, weathered looking man stepped forward and gripped Angus by the hand. Angus recognised him as John Dunlop, a crofter and a senior elder from a neighbouring church

'Mr Munro!' he exclaimed. 'So good of you to come all this way to join us, especially in the extreme weather conditions we are experiencing just now.'

Some years ago, John's married daughter had moved into the parish where Angus ministered, and when visiting his daughter he always attended church. A very devout man with a strong, compelling faith, he had served with the Scots Grey in the Battle of Waterloo. He was badly wounded when his brigade went to rescue their Commander who, with several of his men, went to take out of action a nearby cannon. Three of his comrades had been killed, and John was badly wounded with severe lacerations to the chest and legs. Not expected to live, his sheer determination and solid belief in God saw him make a complete recovery. The experience of being on the victors' side left him with a new mission to serve his church and ensure the full Gospel was proclaimed.

'I'm just amazed at the number of people here,' said Angus.

'Aye, what a multitude!' John replied. 'Some say there are around two thousand people here. Surely the Lord is making his purpose known to us.'

He turned to Angus.

'I've arranged for one of our young men seated in the back pew in the church to give up his place for you. It won't hurt him to stand,' he winked.

The church was full.

Angus took his seat next to an old couple who gave him a warm smile and then continued to look expectantly forward

Two minsters and an Elder were sitting at a mahogany communion table below the pulpit. Sitting to one side was Mr Edwards, the proposed incumbent. One of the ministers Angus didn't recognise. This man continually gazed around the congregation, giving him the impression of an auctioneer looking for the next bidder.

Suddenly the eyes of the congregation settled on John Dunlop slowly walking towards the front of the church. The assembled ministers looked anxiously at each other.

John cleared his throat and, opening a piece of paper, turned to them and said:

'The people of this parish and presbytery earnestly beg you to avoid the desecration of the ordinance of this ordination that is to take place here today. If you decide to disregard this representation, we do solemnly declare in the presence of the Great and only Head of the church, the Lord Jesus Christ, we do repudiate the decision on the preferred ordination of Mr Edwards and his appointment as minister of this church.

'We further declare, if proceedings go ahead, this will invoke the most dishonest act done to religion and cause a cruel injury to the spiritual interests of a united Christian congregation.'

John folded the piece of paper, turned to the congregation, stood for about a minute and walked slowly back down the aisle.

Angus found the scene that followed deeply moving.

In one body the congregation rose; they gathered the bibles that had lain on the pew shelves for generations and walked in a quiet but determined manner out of the church. There was many a tear on the faces of the men and women who passed Angus.

The ministers at the front remained seated, and watched on in silence.

The Manor House – A Novel

By Pam Rowe

Chapter 1

The year was 1912 and Ivy Winter was in the flat above the public house known as the *Cock and Sparrow* in Tottenham, London, as they were licenced victuallers and had owned the pub since they were married five years ago. The clock on the mantelpiece pointed to six o'clock and there was a roaring fire in the grate complimenting the homely room. She was sitting on the comfortable suite that was positioned near the fire where the couple could relax while keeping an eye on the time, as the hours spent at the bar were long and unrelenting.

Her thoughts were re-living the day's events. It had started so well, with the anticipation of Ivy seeing the doctor in the morning - she was eight months pregnant - and then she and her husband John spending the rest of the day choosing a pram and a cot for the bab, plus items of clothes to complete the layette. Ivy had made a couple of night dresses and knitted two matinée coats, but that was all that had been prepared for the oncoming birth of their first born.

On arriving at the doctors, he had greeted

her with his usual bright smile and words of encouragement before asking how she was feeling, asking her to get on the couch so that he could examine her and listen to the baby's heartbeat. He examined the position the baby was laying in the womb and reached for the foetal stethoscope and positioned it on her tummy to count the heartbeats. As he did, his usual happy face took on a grave expression and he turned to Ivy.

'I'm so sorry, Ivy, but I cannot hear your baby's heartbeat. Get dressed and we will talk about it then.'

Ivy could not believe the news as she got down from the couch to sit in a chair near the doctor's desk.

'Please doctor,' she said, 'can my husband come in now so that he understands the position we are in?'

'I'll go and fetch him,' the doctor said, as he made his way to the surgery door and going to the waiting room to fetch John.

They both entered the surgery again and John noticed the anguished look on Ivy's pale face.

'What's up doc?' he joked, trying to keep the mood light.

'As you know,' said the doctor, 'I've just examined Ivy, and there's no heartbeat as far as I can hear, at present. There are a number of reasons for this - which could mean the baby is still alive; but also a big chance that the foetus has died in the womb. I'm so sorry, John, to have to tell you this.'

The news hit John as hard as it had hit Ivy, but he managed to contain his stress.

'What's the next step, doc?' he asked.

'Well,' said the doctor, 'I would like to start your wife's labour off to-morrow morning at Queen Charlottes Hospital.'

Ivy had been booked for a home delivery, and the thought of a hospital admission was an extra blow to her.

Both John and Ivy left the surgery in silence, both sharing their shock and upset by holding each other tightly as they made their way home instead of going shopping – a trip they'd both looked forward to so much because they had been saving hard to buy equipment needed for the little one.

The rest of the day had been a blur for them as they tried to silently come to terms with the situation and John had spent so long letting the family know, as although he was an only child, Ivy had two married sisters and two brothers who were all awaiting news of the oncoming event, as the baby would have been the first grandchild and niece or nephew for them all.

Now, as night approached, they both had to get back to their normal routine by opening the bar with the exception that John insisted that Ivy stay upstairs and rested because of her pending ordeal of the next day.

The long hours of the evening passed by slowly for them and, at eleven, Ivy made her way downstairs to the bar to help clear up and wash the glasses ready for the next day. They both then turned the lights out and locked the door before returning upstairs for their usual cup of cocoa by the embers of the fire before going to bed.

Chapter 2

It was the early hours of the morning.

John was sound asleep, but Ivy was awoken by tummy pains.

She got out of bed to go to the bathroom to find that her waters had broken and she was in the first stages of labour. She awoke John, who got out of bed quickly, donned his clothes and went to summon the midwife who they both knew well because she had been visiting the couple regularly during the ante-natal period.

Ivy managed to collect the bundle of newspapers and mackintosh sheet she had prepared several months before and laid them on the bed.

The midwife arrived and John had told her of the horror of the doctor's visit the day before, and she greeted Ivy with her usual friendliness - but added empathy - before speaking.

'Hello Ivy. I'm here now, we can do this, just relax and do as I say and we'll be fine.'

In the meantime, John went downstairs and telephoned the doctor to inform him of the latest situation.

Ivy laboured during the night, with the support and encouragement of the midwife, while the doctor made arrangements for his partner to cover surgery and his receptionist to postpone other appointments for a later time.

On his arrival at the *Cock and Sparrow* he

examined Ivy once again and found that the baby had turned as the labour had progressed, so he decided to check the foetal heart once again. To his astonishment he heard the heartbeat once again, but did not alert either the midwife or the parents immediately as he did not want to give them false hope at this critical time.

At ten thirty of the morning of 28th April, a baby girl came into the world and after a very short time began to scream the house down - much to the surprise and joy of the parents and others in the room.

Later, after Ivy was made comfortable and her general health checked, the baby was bathed in the sink and dressed in one of the nightdresses and maternity coats there were at hand. This was followed by the dilemma of where to put the baby, and it was decided that the best option was to empty a drawer from the bedroom suite and make up a bed for the baby until a suitable cot and pram could be purchased, together with other necessities that should have been bought the day before.

The day then took on some normality with John opening the pub and Ivy snuggling down and getting some well-earned rest before the midwife returned in the evening to check all was well.

During the afternoon, Ivy's mother arrived from Rochester to care for the family over the next couple of weeks, or until Ivy could resume normal household duties after her lying-in period was over. She greeted her daughter with excitement and love and growing anticipation of meeting her first grandchild. She peered into the drawer at the now sleeping baby and it was love at first sight. This little bundle of joy that everyone feared would never live was here and looking so beautiful in the fading light.

During the evening, the midwife returned and checked Ivy, giving her a blanket bath and making sure that the baby suckled at the breast. She also weighed the baby and found she was good weight - at seven pounds - for an eight month duration, then made her farewells and said she would be back in the morning.

In the meantime, John had found help to take over the day to day running of the pub to enable him to spend more time with his wife and mother-in-law until they were back to normal once again.

A very weary John climbed the stairs to the flat with the anticipation of cuddling his new daughter for the first time and telling his wife how proud he was of her and how much he loved her. He was a very gentle man, although he was large in stature and very tall, with a mop of black hair and angular features. One might even say handsome, although he would never admit to that himself.

As he entered the flat he heard his mother-in-law in the kitchen preparing a late tea.

He said *Hello* and that he was home for the rest of the evening. He then went into the bedroom to find Ivy cuddling the baby having given her her feed earlier on when the midwife was present.

John moved a small kitchen table into the bedroom so they could all be together at mealtimes. They ate mainly in silence, as everyone's thoughts were on the future and also the happenings of the day that had been intermingled with sadness followed by great joy and tiredness.

As they finished their meal, and the washing up and clearing had been done, it seemed the next important thing to do was to think of a name for this small bundle that had created so much havoc over the past forty eight hours. At last it was concluded that she should be called Vera Ivy May Walker:

Vera, meaning *Truth*.

The truth of the matter being that she should not be here at all.

Ivy, after her mother and grandmother's names.

And May, being a favourite aunt's name.

These decisions having been made they all decided it was time for their usual cocoa drink followed by some well-earned rest and sleep.

Chapter 3

The following days passed smoothly for Vera's family. A cot had been bought and a routine was established. Vera continued to thrive and take her place within the family unit. Both parents were besotted with her and her every need was given, from parenting and general care to endless hours of cuddling, loving and taking her for walks within the area of the *Cock and Sparrow* in her newly acquired perambulator.

Her grandmother stayed in Tottenham for a further three weeks before returning to Rochester. She idolized Vera, and played a part that every grandparent should by helping out her daughter and son-in-law, passing on the hints she had learned while bringing up her own family of three girls and two boys.

Other equipment for Vera was soon purchased, and as she grew the usually tidy lounge - with its pretty wallpaper and several pictures hanging on the picture rails - took on a different personality due to the ever increasing amount of toys showered on this favourite grandchild and niece. The parquet floor was an ideal surface for the baby girl to take her first steps and later to push her dolls' pram about while dressing and undressing her favourite dolls.

Over the next year Vera became even

more appealing. Her features developed, so that she had most prominent penetrating brown eyes and golden curls that over the year were growing quickly and would eventually reach her waist.

She sat up at six months and also cut her first tooth.

Walking was established at eleven months, so that when she reached her first birthday she was a bright and happy child, very alert and interested in her surroundings and the people within her circle .

She was spoiled - on her frequent visits to the pub downstairs - by customers, and also by her idolizing grandmother who visited Tottenham regularly. Vera was also taken to Rochester to integrate with the rest of the family who had also taken her into their hearts.

The public bar remained busy and all went fairly uneventfully, with Vera spending half of her life in Tottenham with her parents and the rest in Rochester in Kent with her grandmother - who called her *Boo Boo*, because as a baby she had never cried, only making a booing sound if asking for attention.

Then came 1914, and World War 1 was declared.

John did not know whether he would be called up, but decided to enlist and leave the *Cock and Sparrow* in the capable hands of his wife and several other bar staff now employed.

Although Ivy missed and worried about him terribly, she had enough to do to pass the days with the responsibility of the pub and every day looking after Vera.

Vera enjoyed her life at the *Cock and Sparrow* with her mother, as London was a very interesting place with its huge parks and numerous shops.

She liked going to Hanleys - a well-known toy shop at the centre of the city. There was also a lot to interest her on her outings because women had to take on the role of their menfolk due to the fact they were all at war. Carriages were seen travelling along the roads and large dray horses pulled wagons to deliver beer to the pubs. High class ladies would be seen in their long dresses and large hats walking along the London Streets going to busy stores like Selfridges, anticipating their next purchase to keep up with the fashion of the day.

The scene was very different in Rochester, with its tranquillity of the countryside, its green leafed trees framing open fields that were growing crops needed to feed the entire nation during wartime. There was a beautiful cathedral in Rochester that Vera loved to go to, which intrigued her with the candles on the alter and the carved heads that were visible by the pews. Sometimes the organ was playing, which filled the space with the haunting sound of a hymn. After visiting the cathedral her next favourite pastime was to find a duck pond and call the ducks over to give them pieces of bread that had been saved by her grandmother for this very purpose. The seaside also was not too far away and both would spend many a happy hour sitting on the shore, Vera building sandcastles while her grandmother watched the waves breaking on the shore, and taking note of the bathing huts that were wheeled onto the beach in which ladies changed into their bathing attire before entering the sea for a gentle swim.

Vera loved running around with the agility and freedom that comes with childhood and took great pleasure in collecting shells that were all different shapes and colours to add to her collection in her bedroom at her grandmother's house.

By this time in her life she had several cousins: called Gypsy, Gwen, Sissi and Baba. There was only two to three years difference in their ages, so many games and dressing up took place when they were all together. Vera also loved her bedtime story, usually made up by her grandmother rather than read out of a book.

Ivy, on the other hand, was well aware of the awful conditions her husband had to cope with every day, with dying men laying about in the muddy, rat-infested trenches. She received letters from him from time to time, expressing the longing he had to return home to the normality of everyday life and enjoy the everyday development of Vera growing up. It was one of those days in 1916 when he was shot through the chest and rushed to the army tent where they operated on him and saved his life. Again he was surrounded by injured men being attended by dedicated nurses and doctors who toiled for many hours giving care and comfort to a lot of ill and frightened men, some only boys missing home as much as he did.

John returned home to continue his convalescence, having been dismissed from the forces due to the nature of his injury. Day by day he grew stronger under the tender care of his wife and the joy of watching his daughter's childish antics making him laugh while at the same time calling her to come and give him a cuddle.

Life went on in this vein until the war ended in 1918, by which time Britain had lost many men but those who did return home were mostly broken and disillusioned only to find their jobs were now being done by women. Although they were welcomed back to employment it caused quite a lot of ill feeling as the women were laid off to return to their old life of staying at home, which became hard as they had enjoyed the freedom, responsibility and company of the women in the workforce.

The pub remained busy and John was able to resume his responsibilities behind the bar again while Ivy stood back and took a secondary role in the everyday running of the pub.

It seemed that the worst was over and the horrors of wartime could be forgotten and Britain could return to its former self, although there had been a definite change in people's outlook to life in general.

Vera grew up in this changing world, until

one day she awoke and did not feel her usual bouncy self. Her mother came into her bedroom wondering why she had not got up and dressed ready for her breakfast. Ivy could see the child was not well and called the doctor, who arrived and examined the little girl. He diagnosed Scarlet Fever and said she would have to be removed to a local fever hospital immediately.

Vera was very upset by this and was bundled into an ambulance and taken to a building that was very dire in appearance: high grey stone walls with small windows were apparent as they entered into the bleak corridors that were highly polished but smelt of disinfectant. Stern nurses ushered her into a ward containing lots of iron beds in rows with the sister's desk at the end of the ward. She was put into a bed next to other children either side who were sleeping. As the day went on she began to feel very ill and did not want to eat. Her parents were not allowed to stay, so she felt very lonely and upset. Days were spent in this ward with nurses and doctors going about their work dressed in gowns over their uniforms and wearing material masks to hide their faces so as not to catch the infections they were treating. No sunlight came through the windows, that were barred from the inside, and the walls were a dirty shade of grey. Vera was not allowed any toys, so she spent her days huddled in her bed, tearful on occasions and longing to see her parents again.

Then one day a doctor came round and examined her only to find that she had now caught Diphtheria on top of the Scarlet Fever. He had diagnosed this because of the membrane that covered her tongue. A decision was made to move her to a side ward, as her prognosis was very poor as it was a well-known fact that around ten thousand plus children died each year as there were no antibiotics or immunisation available.

They brought screens around her while an alternative bed was organised and she was then moved into the side ward and shut in the room as it was glass partitioned. She felt even lonelier here. The days passed and she became even more ill, before beginning to improve and her symptoms subsided. Both illnesses so close together had left her very weak and she had lost a lot of weight; her heart had been impaired and on her discharge her parents were told she would need a lot of rest and a long convalescence before her general health became normal again. She returned home to the familiar surroundings she had so missed while in hospital.

She gradually began to gain strength and it was decided that she could be moved to Rochester, as London was very grimy and smoke-filled, and it was hoped that the purer air of Rochester would aid her recovery.

While she was in Rochester, Ivy and John thought long and hard about their lives. The brewery had told them that there was a great public house coming available for sale in Datchet known as The Manor Hotel that included some rooms that were suitable for an overnight stay. They decided that they would go and look at it, as London had seemed to lose its glamour for them and if the Manor was suitable they would consider the move very seriously.

CPSIA information can be obtained
at www.ICGtesting.com
Printed in the USA
BVOW03s0844071216

470033BV00014BA/177/P